A College Affair

Murder at Savan College near Boston:
Intruder, Student, Administration, or Staff?

William J Farrell

Order this book online at www.trafford.com
or email orders@trafford.com

Most Trafford titles are also available at major online book retailers.

Printed in the United States of America.

ISBN: 978-1-4907-1678-7 (sc)
ISBN: 978-1-4907-1680-0 (hc)
ISBN: 978-1-4907-1679-4 (e)

Library of Congress Control Number: 2013918296

Trafford rev. 12/11/2013

 www.trafford.com

North America & international
toll-free: 1 888 232 4444 (USA & Canada) ,
fax: 812 355 4082

CONTENTS

This book is dedicated to my wife Patricia.

CHAPTER ONE

Arthur Pierce was always fascinated with John F. Kennedy. He remembered the time when he was a kid watching the parade on Bunker Hill Street in Charlestown where he was brought up. Kennedy was marching in the parade that day in an effort to get votes for the House of Representatives from the Charlestown Congressional District. There were many other politicians marching in the parade, and they were attempting to get votes too. The parade was held on June 17th which was the date set aside to remember the Battle of Bunker Hill. Many people in Charlestown, who prefer to be called "Townies" if they were born there, considered the 17th of June a bigger holiday than Christmas or their New Year's Eve celebration. They even celebrated the night before the 17th of June at the Sullivan Square playground that they called "The Neck". The 17th of June carnival was held at the "Neck" and people from all over the city played games, rode on the various rides, and many young kids would drink there in an effort to prove their immerging adulthood.

Pierce was retired after spending 30 years teaching at Savan, a small college in the Boston area that was first funded by a grant from John D. Savan in 1845. He remembered his time teaching and the events that shaped his life. Before he came to Savan, he had taught both Latin and English at one of the local high schools in the area.

He thought about Kennedy often, particularly the assassination in Texas. He remembered that day with clarity. It was as though the assassination had happened only yesterday. But on this day, he was thinking about his teaching at Savan College. He was filled with pride at being a college teacher even though his status was that of an instructor. He looked forward to the day when he would be called "professor."

On his first day teaching, he was very apprehensive when he entered the classroom. There were forty students in his class. They had all signed up for the class that was entitled "Family." Some of the students signed up for this class because of the interest that they had about the family and how it was constructed in America and what the various religions in the United States taught about family matters and their dynamics. Others had signed up because they had room in their schedule; still others signed up for the course because a new teacher was teaching it.

He began his first lecture by introducing himself. "Good morning. My name is Mr. Pierce. Unless I give you permission, please refer to me by Mr. Pierce. We will get along better that way. I will pass out an outline of the topics that we will be looking at this morning, plus a word of the day together with an expression of a famous person, and I will also include whatever assignments there are for the next class that we have. I will pass out an outline to you every day that we meet. It's important for you to keep these outlines in one of your folders. That way you might use them to better prepare for our examinations. Of course, the words and expressions are free. They will not be included in any test that might be assigned. After I pass out these outlines, we will introduce ourselves. As I have said, my name is Mr. Pierce. I will read the names of the people here and ask you a few questions. This way we can break the ice."

He walked up and down the aisles of the classroom handing out his outlines. He noticed that there were about an equal number of male and female students who had signed up for the class. He finished handing out the outlines, and then he went through the attendance form that he had picked up at the registrar's office. He began reading the names that were on it.

When a student answered to his or her name, he would ask the student where he or she was from and why he or she was taking this course. Some of the responses were humorous.

"Mr. Anderson?"

"Here, sir."

"How are you today? Where are you from?"

"I'm fine sir and I'm from Springfield, Mass. Thanks for inquiring about my health, how are you today?"

"I'm fine."

He preceded going down the list of the forty students who had signed up for the course and he finally came to the last name in the list.

"Mr. Shaw? How are you today? Why are you taking this course?"

"I'm feeling ok. How about you, how are you feeling?"

"I'm just fine as I have said to the students who have already inquired about my health. Again, may I ask you why you are taking this course?"

"I heard it was a gut," he said smilingly. All of the other students in the class laughed at his response.

"I assure you, sir it is not a gut." Pierce responded sternly, but he was a bit embarrassed at what Shaw had said. "Let's begin by looking at a bit of anthropology."

He began his lecture while the students took notes. He talked about the theories of William Graham Sumner and proceeded to discuss the evolution of the institution of the family as necessary for society. He noticed that even Mr. Shaw was interested in what he had to say. Soon the bell rang. When the students were leaving, Shaw approached Pierce and apologized for his wise response to Pierce's question when he called role. Pierce, as graciously as he could, accepted Shaw's apology.

Pierce left the classroom and went back to his office. He closed the door to his office and breathed a sigh of relief that his first class was over. Now, he thought, he had to prepare his next class.

"I thought teaching was supposed to be easy," he said to himself as he sat in the chair in front of his desk and began his preparations.

After his last class of the day, he decided that it was time to go home. He left the building and proceeded to go to his car. The sun was still shining and left a bright red color in the sky as though the sky and the color left by the sun were both painted by some artist. The red color bounced off the buildings that were in the rear of the building where Pierce had his office. He got into his car and drove away from the campus and headed home. He lived in a small apartment near the college. When he drove off, Robert Shaw was in his dormitory talking to his friends.

"Hey Steve, how were your classes today?" Bob Shaw asked his roommate Steve Long who had a different class at the time when Shaw was taking the course with Pierce. His class was taught by Professor Mark Bourque who had a reputation of being a very tough teacher.

"They were fine. I understand that you gave Pierce a hard time today. I'm not in the class like the rest of these clowns but I heard what you said," he replied to the amusement of the other students who had crowded into the room.

Bill Galvin was there together with Mark Iota and Barry Sparks. Mark Iota had to share a room with Galvin and Sparks. Although 'trips" or three students in a dormitory was a policy with the school, Iota didn't like it.

Bob Shaw, who was a big man, shared his room with Steve Long, who was also not very big. Physically, they both were rather plain and ordinary looking. Bill Galvin was also plain and ordinary looking; while Barry Sparks was rather good looking, Mark Iota was the most handsome of all of them. Mark was odd in his personality though, and he was also a homosexual, as was Shaw. Both of them had an ongoing relationship. The other guys were not aware of this and they all hung out together. It was a time when Archie Bunker was a popular actor on television and when people were playing Scrabble at home when they were not watching television.

Long was in a separate class than the others. His class met at the same time as the others but in a different room. He had different career goals. He had interests that the other guys didn't have.

"No, I didn't give him a hard time. I just said that I was taking his class because I heard it was a gut." The other students in the room began laughing and they continued to laugh, especially Barry Sparks.

"Sure. You didn't mean anything," Sparks replied as he continued laughing while the other students, who had joined him in laughing, stopped. Now they only smiled at what Shaw had said.

After they gabbed for a few minutes, they decided that they would leave Shaw's room and go to The Lamppost, the bar down the street from the campus. Before they left the room, they looked at their fake IDs to make sure that they had the correct date that indicated they were twenty one. They all looked of age. When they got to the bar, Long went up to the bartender ordering five beers. The others took a table near the window.

"Let's see your ID," the bartender said gruffly.

"Sure, no problem," Long replied as he fished into his pocket and took out his laminated ID.

"Ok, you're good, how about the other guys?"

"They're all good too."

The bartender shrugged his shoulders as he drew the beers from the spigot. He was not really concerned about the ages of the boys since the investigator had been by on the day before. The job of the investigator was to determine if the barrooms that he was charged to investigate were in compliance with the law that required patrons to show their ID proving that they were 21. The bartender was not concerned since the investigator came to his bar only once during the year and he had already checked Long's ID.

Steve Long carried the beers to the table where the other four students were sitting. He carried two mugs at a time to the table and then two more before he sat down with his own beer.

"Thanks for the help, guys. I really appreciate it."

"No sweat," Shaw responded half in jest.

They all took their mugs, and after proposing a toast to the school year talked to one another about their plans for the future. Iota said that he wanted to go to law school when he finished his AB requirements at Savan. Both Shaw and Long said that they had not made any plans. The other two were vague about what they wanted to do after they had graduated. Galvin said that he might go into business for himself and Sparks indicated that he was leaning toward social work.

"That's all well and good, but aren't we supposed to be thinking about pulling a prank," Shaw said as he sipped his beer.

"Isn't that kind of old fashioned?" Iota replied.

"Not at all, I know that a lot of people feel that way but it isn't true. The truth of the matter is that freshmen are expected to pull pranks," Shaw answered. "What do you other guys think?"

"I'm not sure. What kind of a prank do you have in mind?" Sparks asked.

"I don't know. I've been thinking about such things as putting silly things on the board when Pierce comes into his class or some other prank. Like when he parks his car. I don't know. Something."

"I know what you're saying. But I don't know what kind of a prank that we could pull off," Galvin responded.

"Neither do I," Shaw indicated as he shuffled his feet. He continued to think about it. His thoughts took over his entire personality or, at least, it appeared that way.

"We'll think of something. Let's drink our beers now that we have them. We'll think of pranks later." Shaw was smiling when he spoke.

All of the boys agreed and they drank their beers. Long finished his before the others and said half pouting and half in jest, "Hey guys, when are you going to finish? I've finished mine. Shall we get more?" They all nodded and Long went back to the bar.

"Let's have five more," he said to the bartender in a glib manner.

"Sure."

He brought the beers back to the table as he had done just a short time ago; at least he thought that it was only a minute or two. This was the first time that he drank anything that might interfere with his thinking about time. He laughed as he stumbled back to the table.

"Here you go guys. Beers for everyone!'

Iota joined in the cheers, but he wished that his glass had a hole in it. He didn't like the taste of beer and he felt full. He was not very comfortable. He decided that he would leave his glass half full on the table.

CHAPTER TWO

When they had finished they went back to their dormitories. Iota left his unfinished glass on the table. The rest had finished their beers before they left the barroom and they began their journey to their new homes. The sun had a funny way of confusing them. It was hiding in the clouds when they went outside, but now it was dancing while it shone on their faces. As they were crossing the street, they began singing the fight song that they had heard the football players on campus sing.

The next day, Pierce entered the classroom. He put his books on the desk, and put his briefcase on the chair that was in front of the desk. He turned around to erase the blackboard and stopped at what he was doing as he looked at the stick figure of a man with an arrow through his body. Below was Pierce's name.

"Don't you like what you see?" Shaw shouted.

Pierce remained silent. His immediate reaction was to ask him who the wise guy was, but, after he thought about it for a very brief moment, he erased the image without saying a word. He then erased the entire blackboard.

"Let's begin. Are there any questions from the last class that we had the first day we met?" He paused and when no hands went up, he proceeded with the lecture that he had prepared.

"The last time was devoted to getting to know one another. I realize that we won't get to know each other before the end of the semester, but it is much easier when we introduce one another at the semester's beginning. We also spoke a little bit about anthropology and the evolution of the family. We also looked at some of Sumner's theories." He said all of this while he went up and down the aisles passing out the outlines that he had prepared for the class. He thought about the fact that he was giving only his second lecture. The thought of this made him feel proud, but on the other hand he felt a bit nervous. The fear of speaking in front of people whether they are students or not, never goes away. When he had finished the lecture, he again asked if there were any questions. Shaw raised his hand.

"Is the assignment that you have indicated on the outline due next class?"

"Yes it is."

"I have a test following this class and I am not alone. Some of the students in this class have the same test. Could we possibly postpone the assignment for next week?"

"No."

"But the guys all have asked me to bring it up and even though the examination is early in the semester, if you give us a break to study for it, it would be appreciated."

"I said 'no'."

"I guess that's it then. Thanks."

"You're welcome. That's all. Class dismissed."

The students quietly filled out of the classroom. When they got to the hall, Shaw turned his head and smilingly said to Galvin and the other students who had followed him, "What a jerk he is."

"He is, but I didn't know that we had a test next class," Galvin said with a surprised look on his face.

"We don't. I was just saying that to get him to postpone his assignment. I don't feel like reading the first hundred pages of the text. Do You?"

"No," Galvin said.

"What about the rest of you guys? Do you want to read a hundred pages before the next class?"

"No," they shouted half in unison, "we don't. It's too much reading this early in the semester. We have other things to do."

"Ok then. I was right in what I asked him? The jerk," Shaw responded.

"Yeah, you were. What are your plans now?" Galvin asked.

"I don't know. I'll think of something," Shaw said.

He then went looking for Long, together with Galvin, Iota and Sparks. They finally found him when he exited the class that he was taking. It was the health class. They told him about what Shaw had said to Pierce and then they walked to the barroom down the street from the campus where they were the other day. The barroom was the habitual place where the students of Savan hung out during the academic year. When the students were not around, the place was comparatively empty.

"Give me five beers," Long said to the bartender.

"You back again? I don't need to see your ID today. I won't ask you about your friends either."

Long took the beers over to the table where the others sat, two beers at a time, just like the other day. Shaw, who had just been applauded by the other students who had crowded in the barroom, took command of the conversation at the table. He responded to the accolades of the other students and then spoke with his friends.

"Here's to Pierce and what he stands for," he said half-jokingly as he raised his glass.

"Yeah, yeah, here's to Pierce," the others chimed in as they raised their glasses.

"What do we do next? That stick figure you drew on the board didn't get too much of a response from him. You really should draw a better figure, Bob. You know you've got the talent." Long took a long haul on his beer and he appeared to be a bit glassy eyed.

"I don't really know," Shaw replied. "I agree that the figure I put on the board was not my best effort. We'll think of something."

He sipped on his beer but his thoughts focused on the next prank that he would pull. Perhaps it should be more intense than just drawing a stick figure on the board. He got more involved with his thinking about it. He got so involved that he stopped speaking. The other guys at the table noticed it.

"He's not talking. Maybe we offended him," Long looked directly at Shaw.

Shaw was engrossed in what to do next. He thought that maybe he could do something with Pierce's office or with his car. He would need the other guys to help him if he did do something bigger than drawing on the blackboard and they would help him do whatever he asked them to do. After all, he was their leader.

Galvin left the table and he joined the rest of the students in singing Savan's fight song. The bartender looked at them as they crowded the bar. He shrugged, smiled a half smile and then went back to what he was doing. The students finished their song;

"We will fight for old Savan till they all come home!"

When they finished the song, they all returned to their table. They started to punch one another on the arm and claimed that their version of the song was superior to anyone else's and that they had sung it better. They said that they were all sober and that the bartender was a clown.

The bartender was an alcoholic. He knew it. He was a member of an AA group and had gone to meetings at least once a week. Serving beers to the students didn't bother him. As a matter of fact, he often mixed drinks for the guests at parties that he had at his home. He made martinis or manhattans for people without wanting to drink himself. It didn't bother him at all even though manhattans and martinis were his drinks of choice when he was out drinking with his friends. Pouring beer from the spigot for college students was not a problem for him.

Shaw, sitting at the table, looked out the window that was beside him. The sun was just setting. It left a faint, pink and red glow in the sky that reflected on the glass that he held in hand. He marveled at nature's way of telling him what to do; at least this was the conclusion that he had come to.

"Hey guys," he shouted," I know what we'll do!"

Galvin came back to the table to listen to what Shaw had to say. The other boys, Iota, Long and Sparks, looked at Shaw curiously.

"I know what we'll do! We'll flood his office!"

"Yeah, sure," Sparks said. "Where are we going to get the water to do that?"

"From the hose outside his office, look, there's a faucet outside his office that we can use. All we have to do is get in. We could break the window that he has, pull the hose through and put it on. Swoosh, his whole office would get wet. We'll be heroes! What do you guys think?"

"Well," Galvin hesitated, "what if we got caught? Think about it. What if someone heard us or heard the glass break when we smashed his window?"

"Nobody's going to hear us. Besides, if we do it late at night and have a, what do you call it . . . . some kind of a gizmo. We've seen these things in the movies. We could place it on the window and then circle it near where the window lock is. We won't make any noise at all. And, of course, we'll do it when the campus security has already checked things out. So, what do you say? Are you with me?"

"I'm still a bit leery, but I'll go along with the plan. But where are you going to get the gizmo?" Galvin asked half-heartedly.

The other boys laughed and said it was a great idea. They thought that they could get the gizmo from the metal shop down the street from the campus. It shouldn't be a problem.

"So that's the plan. We'll meet tonight at midnight and do it!" Shaw looked at the other boys with a churlish smile on his face.

They left the barroom and went back to their dorm rooms. Shaw told Long that he was a bit tired and needed to take a nap. He lay down on his bed and went right to sleep. Long thought it might be the beers that he drank that made him tired; although it might have been the plan that he came up with. Long didn't know.

CHAPTER THREE

That night, after getting the "gizmo" from the shop in the afternoon, they all met at midnight outside of Shaw's dormitory. They were all dressed differently. One of the boys had a cap, the others were bare headed. One wore jeans while the others had khakis on. But they were all intent at accomplishing Shaw's plan of soaking Pierce's office.

Stealthily, they went to the rear of Pierce's office where the hose was attached to the water line. After groping for a long while and arguing with Shaw about how it should be done, they pulled out the gizmo and cut a circle in the window just above were the latch was. When they finished cutting the circle in the window, Shaw gingerly pushed the window lock up and opened the window. When he opened it, they all crawled in.

"You go out and attach the hose," Shaw told Iota. Iota went out again through the window and attached the hose to the faucet. But he resented Shaw telling him what to do.

"This should be fun," Shaw told the others as he put the lights on.

"Hey, someone will see the lights," Long whispered.

"No they won't. Besides even if they do, they'll think that Pierce was working late or was coming back to look for a book or something. After all, it's after midnight," Shaw answered. "Security has already been here."

"Oh, ok, ok, let's get to it," Long answered nervously

When they got the hose inside the office, they shouted to Iota to turn the water on. He did and then came back into the room through the window. Then they all began their work. First they set the hose on the spray position. Next, they sprayed all the book cases and the books that Pierce read and took such delight in. Then they sprayed the walls, Pierce's desk and the floor. The floor had a wall to wall carpet on it which absorbed the water very quickly and hopefully prevented it from running out into the hall. The boys, especially Shaw, laughed when they were spraying the water on everything. Shaw had the special onus of being the leader of the guys, the planner of what they had done and the one who would be responsible for their escape.

"Ok, we're finished. The books, the floor and walls are all soaking wet. So is his desk. We should leave now," he said.

"Let's go," they all said together.

They left the flooded room through the open window after throwing the hose out. First Galvin, then Iota followed by Sparks and Long. Shaw was the last one to leave after he looked at the walls and floor. His gaze was focused on the floor as he came to the window. He thought that the water might run into the hallway.

"I can't worry about that. Let's get crakin' guys. Let's get out of here and head back to the dorms," Shaw said as he climbed out the window.

They proceeded to leave the building and went back to their dormitories. Once there, they went to their respective rooms and went to bed. Shaw could not fall asleep. "We did it. We flooded that jerk's office! Won't he be surprised when he comes in tomorrow! Won't he be surprised!" Shaw said to Long, his roommate.

CHAPTER FOUR

When Bob, the janitor, came in the next morning he was surprised at what he saw. He came in very early, around 4:30am, and was anxious to have his day go by quickly. He had made plans to see his grandchildren that afternoon. But today would be quite different for him.

Bob opened the door to Pierce's office and he squished over the carpet. He looked at the walls and the books and thought to himself that Pierce would be very angry at what happened to his office, "Holy shit," he said out loud, "Pierce will blow his stack when he sees this."

He walked through the office and looked at the damaged books and the still wet carpet and wall. His first thought was to call the office and tell them what had happened. After thinking about it, he decided that the fewer people who knew about it the better.

"My goodness, they, whoever did this, did a really good job at ruining things. Somebody has to pay. I'm not going to clean this place up though. It's not my job to do this kind of thing. Besides, I'll wait till Pierce comes in."

Pierce finally came in while Bob continued to vacuum the other offices on his floor. There were several offices other than Pierce's on the same floor that Bob took care of. When he saw Pierce come in he stopped his vacuuming,

He went up to him and said. "I have some bad news for you. Somebody really messed up your office. They apparently took the hose and doused your carpet and walls and all your books."

"What!"

"They really ruined things for you."

"I don't believe it, let's see."

They both headed for Pierce's office. When they got there, some of the water was coming out on the corridor floor.

"Oh shit," Bob said, "I better take care of this."

Pierce anxiously took his office keys from his pocket and opened the door. He stood dazed at what he saw. All of his books were soaked as well as the bookcases and the walls. The carpet still had puddles of water on it.

"I can't believe what I'm seeing," he said "I can't believe it".

He turned to Bob and asked him what had happened. Bob shrugged and said that he didn't know.

"Someone obviously came into your office last night and doused the place. Look at the glass on the floor. They must have cut their way in and opened your window. They must have used the hose outside to do all this damage."

"I'll be a son-of-a-bitch," Pierce screamed out loud.

He got some of his notes from his desk. They were not damaged. Then he left his wet office. Fuming with anger, he ran across the campus bumping into students unapologetically. Ordinarily, he would notice the vibrant colors of the trees with their leaves spouting colors of yellow and red illuminated by the sun, but now he didn't notice them. He was angry, he was mad. When he got to the building where he had his class, he ran up the stairs and entered the classroom. His students were already there.

"OK. Who's the wise guy? I know it's one of you!"

"What do you mean?" asked the pretty girl who sat in the front of the class.

"Whatever I said! Who's the wise ass? My office is destroyed! Someone invaded it last night and they flooded the place! They soaked all my books, the walls, the carpet, everything!" He thought that he knew who was responsible.

"They soaked the whole place? That's a shame," Shaw said mockingly.

Pierce looked directly at him and angrily accused him of soaking his office.

"I know you did it!"

"How can you say that? I was in my dormitory room all night. I was asleep! Just ask my roommate. He's not in this class. He's too smart," he said as he turned around and looked at the rest of the class.

"Sure, he was asleep," Galvin said.

"I'll bet! You probably were there with him!" Pierce was still angry when he said that. "I'm too upset to teach today. Class dismissed."

Students huddled around Pierce when he said that he was too upset to teach. They all felt sorry for him. The ones who had been involved in the soaking left the classroom. When they were a little way from the room, they joined Shaw in laughing.

"We certainly showed him," Shaw said. There was pride in his voice when he said that.

"We did. We certainly did, didn't we! Now we have to think about not getting caught." Iota showed some concern. One could tell that he didn't like Shaw.

"We won't! Hey, what do you other guys think? Mark, you're really too worried. You worry about everything."

"I don't! I'm just concerned. That's all."

Galvin and Sparks agreed. Long would too if he was in the class. The three students in the class were still smiling about what they had done. It was fun to ruin Pierce's office they thought.

"Of course we won't be caught. We won't. Who's going to squeal? Not me. I wouldn't' tell him anything! What a dork he is! I can't stand Pierce, the way he talks and all the stuff that he says." Galvin was still angry at the assignment that Pierce had given to the class. Reading was not his favorite thing.

Pierce was still in the classroom talking to the students who were gathered around him. They were all sympathetic about the loss of his books and the damage that had been done to his property. One of them in particular was nearly in tears. It was the girl who sat in front of the class; her name was Irene Doherty.

"You must be terribly upset. I know that I would be if that had happened to me." She could hardly hold back her tears.

"Thanks. I'll get by," Pierce responded.

"What were they thinking? Why did they do it, do you have any idea?" William Griffin asked. Megan was very concerned.

"No, I don't." Pierce answered.

"They'll get caught, whoever they are, they'll get caught," Robert Alton said bowing his head.

"I hope that they do." Pierce began to leave the room. "I really appreciate the concern that you guys have shown."

The students who were gathered around Pierce broke up their group and left with him. Some of them were shaking their head; others were upset at what had been done to Pierce's office but they didn't show it. Then they all went their separate ways.

Two days later, Pierce went to his class. "Ok, everybody, take out your reader. Today we are going to look at the first hundred pages and I'm going to ask you some questions."

"Boy, that's interesting," Shaw said.

"I'll be the judge of that. But why don't you go see the Dean of Discipline? Why don't you. I have made an appointment with him for you," Pierce smiled.

"Sure, I'll keep your silly appointment. I have nothing to hide."

Shaw got up and took his books and left the room. He hastily went to the Dean of Discipline's office. When he got there, he had to wait for his appointment. The Dean's secretary smiled at him and he smiled back acknowledging her greeting.

"Do I have to wait long?" he asked.

"No, he'll be with you momentarily."

The Dean came out of his office and greeted Shaw. He was a big man standing well over six feet tall and he weighed over two hundred and fifty pounds. His name was Robert Lane.

"Good to see you," he said extending his hand.

"Good to see you too."

"Come into my office."

"Sure."

They proceeded to go into the Dean's office. The Dean of Discipline was called "Big Guy" by the students at Savan. They would often tease the other guys by saying that the "Big Guy" wanted to see them. Or if a girl was involved, they would say the same thing to her, but with more respect. When they both got inside, the Dean sat behind his big desk and Shaw took the seat in front of the desk. He leaned forward and asked the Dean why Pierce wanted him to see the Dean of Discipline. He pretended that he was concerned about this meeting.

"Why do you want to see me?"

"Mr. Pierce made a complaint and he made an appointment for you. He said that you were the one responsible for all the damage that was done to his office. It's a pretty serious charge. Were you responsible? Were you the one?"

"Of course not," Shaw said feigning anger.

"Well he said so. He also said that you were a pest in class."

"So who are you going to believe a first year student or a first year teacher? It's his word against mine. And if the college pursues this, I will sue." Shaw appeared to be very angry.

The Dean didn't want the college to be sued. He thought about what Shaw had just said and that there were too many suits already against colleges. He thought of all the suits that there were and that they were all manufactured.

"Ok, I'll be watching you. If you get into any kind of trouble, even if it's a minor infraction, you'll be kicked out of school. Do you understand? Am I getting through to you?" He was quite clear when he said this.

"Can I go now?"

"Go. Get out of my office!"

"Ok, ok I'm going. It's been fun talking with you though."

"You really are a wise ass aren't you?"

"No, I'm just a freshman who is just learning the ropes of college life," he said half mockingly.

"Sure. Sure you are. Get the hell out of my office!"

CHAPTER FIVE

Shaw left the Dean's office with a smile on his face. He left the campus and went to the Lamppost, the bar down the street where the other students had congregated. Galvin was waiting to hear how the Dean acted. He, together with Iota, Sparks and Long, was very anxious to hear what was said and how Shaw responded. They were all waiting when Shaw came into the bar. All the students applauded. Some of them had to put their mugs down when they did but they didn't seem to mind this small inconvenience. They were ready to join the others in applauding Shaw. When they all stopped applauding, Shaw looked around the barroom and then he spoke.

"Thanks, thanks gentlemen. You are too kind. I come here to tell you that everything is ok. The Dean had no recourse available to him. He could either accept my word that I did nothing wrong or he could accept what Pierce had said. It was my word against his and I threatened to sue the college if they blamed me for the unfortunate problem that Pierce had. Colleges don't like the threat of being sued. Remember that."

Galvin was relieved, so were Iota, Sparks and Long. Long went up to the bar and ordered five beers. This time, while the other boys sat down at their table, the bartender did not ask him for an ID nor did he speak to him.

When they were all seated, Shaw began speaking.

"Well, we showed them who was boss! I really am glad that we pulled it all off."

"We sure did," answered Iota half in jest.

"We did indeed," Shaw responded. "Now what?"

"I guess we'll just have to think of something else," Galvin said.

"Yeah, let me think." Shaw was ready now to do anything that would get him in trouble. He didn't want to go to the Dean of Discipline's office again. He added him to the people on campus that he had no use for.

While he was thinking, a girl came up to him and began speaking.

"Hi, my name is Megan Sullivan. How you doin'?"

"I'm just fine. How're you doin'?"

"I'm fine too. I've been watching you. Listen, I was wondering if you had a date for the formal. If not, would you like to go with me?"

Practically everyone in the barroom laughed when she said that. They were intent on listening to what she had to say to Shaw. The boys sitting at his table were particularly amused. Iota made a comment about the choice that the girl had made. The other guys looked amused.

"Sure, I'm not fussy. I'll go to the stupid formal with you. I have nothing else to do. When is it anyhow?" Shaw looked serious when he said that.

"It's tomorrow night. I'm in Halley Hall, Room 201. You can pick me up at 7:30 if you can. Is that ok?"

"Sure. I'll be there at 7:30. Now you can go back to your friends, Megan. I really don't mind."

All the guys at the table cheered Shaw when he said that.

"You sure are a funny guy. Really you are," Iota exclaimed.

The girl left Shaw's table and went back to her friends. When she got to the table, she sat down with them. The girls were dressed in casual attire, very casual, some wearing jeans, others wearing khakis. She was smiling when she told them that Shaw had agreed to pick her up and go to the formal with her. All the girls at the table began to giggle. They giggled because they all knew that Shaw would go to pick Megan up but she would not be there.

"What a trip!" Moira Larkin said.

"It certainly is a real big one! OMG!" Gabriella LaRocha responded.

"Right," Megan replied, "when he comes to pick me up, I'll be gone."

"He really will be so surprised! OMG," Moira said.

"Yeah, he'll be surprised," Samantha Lavine said.

All of the girls at the table agreed. Bob Shaw would come to Halley Hall and knock on the door at Room 201 tomorrow night and nobody would answer. He surely would know that he was stood up. The girls all felt badly for Mr. Pierce. They thought that he was nice in class, that he explained things well and that Shaw had no right to do what he did in class and what he had done in Professor Pierce's office. They all knew that he was guilty. They knew that he had been the one who flooded the office and destroyed his books. They felt sorry for Mr. Pierce when they gathered around him with the other students after their class and tried to be as solicitous as they could.

Meanwhile, Shaw was boasting to his friends at his table that he could get any girl that he wanted. He was a very good basketball player. He was also a good looking young man. He stood a bit over six feet tall and weighed about 180 pounds. He had a very outgoing personality. When he walked, he had a regal stance about him and was confident in everything that he did. He was so confident that he bothered almost everyone that he came into contact with.

"You the man," Iota shouted half in jest.

"Yeah, you are!" Long said while the others at the table nodded their heads in agreement.

They finished their beers and left the barroom. All but Iota walked back to their dorms where they entered into their respective rooms. When Shaw got to his room, he smiled to himself and said to Long, his roommate, that he was going to his first formal in college and that he was going with a very cute young coed. Long was only partially interested. He looked away.

The girls left the barroom too. They began singing as they left. They sang the song that they had learned from practicing the song that they heard the football team singing. It was the official song of Savan College and the same one that the students had sung at the bar. As they climbed the hill that led up to the campus, they began teasing Megan for her "date" with Shaw. They reminded her that she was going to stand him up.

"You sure know how to pick 'em," Gabriella said.

"She sure does," Moira replied.

They finally came to the entrance to the campus and went directly to their rooms in Halley Hall. They got there and went into their rooms. When they got to their rooms, Megan said to her roommate, Gabriella that she was tired and needed to lie down. She blamed the beers that she had at the barroom. But, she almost always napped in the afternoon.

Shortly after waking up she looked, half glassy-eyed, around the room. She expected Gabriella to also be lying down. But Gabriella was sitting at the only desk in the room doing what seemed to Megan to be the assignment for that day. But it was not her assignment.

"What are you doing?" Megan asked.

"Not much. I'm writing my mother at home."

But she wasn't. Instead, she was penning a plan to get Shaw. She dropped her pen and stopped writing when Megan approached the desk. What she had already written was a plan to bring shame to Shaw and his friends by not having Megan in the room when Shaw called. But Megan had already made up her mind that when Shaw knocked on her door, she would not be there.

Megan changed her clothes and asked Gabriella if she was going to change hers before they went out. When Gabriella said that she was comfortable wearing what she had on, they left the room and went down the hall to get Moira and Samantha, Moira's roommate. Moira had been designing a plan to embarrass Shaw as well. Girls do that sort of thing. They generally stick together. Moira asked Samantha if she was ready to go out again and Samantha said that she was. Their room was just down the hall from Megan. All four girls went to the barroom again. When they got there, they went to the table that they had just left while Megan went up to the bar to get beers for all of them.

"You back again?" asked the bartender.

"Yeah, could you give me four beers?"

"I'll need to check your ID," the bartender said with a smile on his face. He knew that he didn't have to check, but he didn't like the girls from Savan.

"I'm just kidding," he said as he poured the beers from the spigot.

When Megan got the beers she took them to the table two in each hand. When she sat down, the girls asked her if she had thought about tomorrow night. Moira, looking directly at her, took the initiative and asked her what she had planned for the evening, what she had intended to do, what her plans were for the "date" that she had.

"What are your plans for tomorrow night? I have sketched out something that I would like you to look at." Moira handed Megan the paper that she had been writing on.

"I have something too," Gabriella said.

The girls all talked about their plans. The other girls laughed when they did. Both compositions arrived at the same conclusion; Shaw would be victimized this time. He would not find Megan when he came to pick her up at her dorm room. He would probably look around, be a bit confused and the girls would get their revenge for Professor Pierce. It would not be the same as when the offenders, probably guys who were led by Shaw, destroyed his office by flooding it. But the girls were content with their plan to stand him up when he came to Megan's room.

"I probably will stay here and get drunk," Megan said to the girls.

"Wow! You really are into it aren't you?" Moira replied.

"She sure is!" Samantha said in reply.

"I guess we will show that moron." Gabriella felt left out of the conversation.

When the girls finished their beers, they got up from the table and left the bar, all but Megan who felt lonely and a bit confused. She decided to stay in the barroom. She bade farewell to the other girls and remained sitting by herself. The barroom was crowded with students from Savan. They seemed, to Megan, to be looking directly at her. One boy, Freddie Chase, came over to her table and sat down. He began to flirt with her. His flirtations were quite obvious. He told Megan that he was a senior and she should feel honored by his attention and should go to the formal tomorrow with him. He obviously didn't have a date. When she refused the invitation, Freddie got very upset.

"I don't understand. Most girls would be delighted to have a senior invite her to the dance tomorrow night. I am shocked at your refusal, really I am." Freddie was a good looking young man. He was tall and well groomed. But Megan was stern in her refusal.

"I really can't. I have plans."

"Ok, you've lost your chance." He got up and left the table.

Megan was not unhappy to see him go. She lifted her glass and drank the rest of her beer. When, she said to herself that she needed another, she decided to get up and go to the bar. She asked the bartender if he would mind filling up her glass.

"Sure, I can do that. I noticed you were still sitting at the table when the other girls left. Can I be of any help? You know that bartenders have a receptive ear. Any problem at all!" He continued to fill Megan's glass with beer as he spoke.

"No thanks. I'll just have another beer." Megan took her glass that was filled to the brim with beer and went back to her table.

CHAPTER SIX

She tried to avoid the stares of the other students, especially Freddie. She got back to her table, sat down and quietly drank her beer. Her thoughts were of Robert Shaw. She didn't have the time or the inclination to think of anything or anybody else, not Freddie nor any of the students who were in the barroom. She was young and beautiful; she may have been only 18 but had the body of a movie star.

Freddie and his friends were sitting at another table. They had a number of beers in front of them. They had been drinking most of the day. Freddie's friends, who were pretty drunk, including John, Bill, Ted and Ray Romano had been staring at Megan during their drinking bout. He finally got up from his seat and went over to Megan's table. The other students who were sitting at their own table began to holler out that Ray's intentions were far from honorable. They said things that they would normally would not say; perhaps it was the beers that they had consumed during their day of drinking.

"Hi there, may I sit down?" he said to Megan.

He sat down anyhow and began his flirtation. He told her that he was a senior and what he wanted to do in life when he graduated. She didn't seem to be interested but after a period of time and a few more sips of her beer, she began to respond to him and to what he was saying. She looked around the room and told Ray that she was only a freshman at Savan and she didn't have any experience at all in talking to seniors.

"I am really impressed that you are a senior and will be going to law school next year. But what does a freshman do when it comes to planning for the future?

Anybody that knew her could immediately tell that she was not being sincere and that she was probably affected by the beers that she had already drunk. Ray responded with words that were aimed at seduction but were not so obvious that Megan would recognize that they were attempts to get her to do his bidding. She was not accustomed to pick up lines. Nothing in her past life prepared her for what Ray was saying, but she was sincere in her responses to his words.

"Shall we get out of here," he asked.

"Where would we go?"

"How about back to your dormitory?"

"Ok." She had made her first blunder.

They got up from the table and left the bar. It was getting dark outside. The first star of the evening was blinking in the sky and the full moon that was predicted for that evening began to show its face. It was getting cooler. In September it gets a bit cooler when the sun goes down. Just then a September star fell from the heavens.

"Oh look, we have a shooting star!" She exclaimed excitedly.

"Yeah, we have them often in Boston."

She innocently took his hand. He felt that this was a sign that she was willing to do what he wanted, that she would go to bed with him. But to her, this is what friends do when they are walking together, especially on a cool September evening; especially when one sees a shooting star. The weather was getting still cooler as they walked back to her dormitory. The moon shone and it made a light that resembled the light of the sun; it made everything look brighter. It shined brightly on Commonwealth Avenue as Ray and Megan made their way back to Savan. They climbed the hill that led them to the campus and to the dormitories. When they got there, they went to Halley Hall, to her room. Gabriella was not there. Ray looked around the room and said that the decorations that she or her roommate had put up were very attractive. He pointed to the bed and said that it was kind of small for both of them.

"What do you mean?" She looked surprised when he said that. The effect of the beers that she drank was wearing off.

"I mean that it will be kind'a small for both of us when we have sex. I roll around a lot."

"What? We aren't having sex! I thought you were a nice young man! You are a senior here at Savan and I thought that you were a nice young man when we talked in the bar! You can leave now. I don't want you in here. Get out! Please! Leave! Now!"

"Ok, ok I'm goin', I'm goin'. Don't get yourself in an uproar. Don't get excited! I'm leaving. Ok?"

Ray left while cursing Megan. He had sex on his mind and he thought that this was his opportunity. But no, no sex nothing like that. When he left, Megan showered and changed her clothes. She thought that she would go down the hall and see Moira and her roommate Samantha before going to bed and see if Gabriella was there. She put on her robe and went down the hall. She knocked on Moira's door and when Moira answered she smiled.

"Megan! What are you doing here? I thought that you would still be at the bar."

"I know. But I changed my mind. Besides I really don't like beer that much and some guy tried to pick me up. He seemed nice. He seemed very nice and he was a senior. But all he wanted was to have sex."

"Come on in, come in. You poor dear, I understand where you're coming from. Guys are like that. All they think about is sex. But you've other things on your mind right now."

"Is Gabby here?"

"No she's not. Just your old friend, Samantha, that's all."

She asked her roommate Samantha what she thought about the whole thing, about standing Shaw up tomorrow night. Moira looked very anxious and was asking Samantha because she needed someone to support her. She began pacing the floor. She said that Shaw would be really upset when he found out that he was being stood up. She looked at Megan and told her about her concern. Megan responded that it was no big deal that lots of guys were stood up.

Robert Shaw went to Room 201 in Halley Hall the following night to pick Megan up. He knocked on her door and waited. He had a cigarette in his mouth and he was dressed up with a black suit, white shirt and a dark tie. When nobody answered, he knocked again. He knocked a third time and when nobody answered, he tried the knob and turned it and he went inside the room. He called her name. He cursed when he realized that Megan was not there. He called her again, this time louder. Then he realized that he was stood up. He looked around the room, dropped his cigarette on the floor and stamped it out.

"Who does she think she is!? Doesn't she know who I am? I'm doing her a favor. She's the one who asked me! The bitch!"

He began to pace up and down the floor. He continued to look around the room and decided that he would go to the dance by himself. All the other guys were there. They went because they wanted to see Shaw bring his date. They would be totally surprised when he showed up by himself he thought.

"First I have to prove that I came to her room and that she was not here. I should take a souvenir of the evening anyhow. I'll show those guys!'

He looked around the room and noticed that she had a small box where she probably hid her jewelry. He went over to the box and opened it. He looked inside and when he found a pair of earrings he took one. Maybe, he thought he should take both of them. But one would be all that he needed. One was enough. He left the other earring in the box.

"Ah, hah, this should do the trick. I'll show the guys an earring and they'll know I was here. I can't let the guys know that I was stood up. Not me! Not Robert Charles Shaw!"

CHAPTER SEVEN

Meanwhile, the guys were at the dance already. They were standing around the punch bowl watching the other students dancing to the music. They thought that this was the place to be. The band was playing very loud music. The guys, who were drinking from the punch bowl, commented that all the girls looked very pretty in their gowns and that the male students looked very handsome in their tuxedos. Quite a few students were standing next to the punch bowl. The female students didn't want any punch. Gabriella LaRocha was there, so were Megan Sullivan, Samantha Lavine and Moira Larkin. They didn't like to drink at dances, they just wanted to dance. Somebody had spiked the punch bowl by putting vodka in it along with the punch that was already there. Occasionally, when a male student walked by, the other students who were standing next to the punch bowl would offer him a drink. If he refused, they would call him names. They commented that if a guy didn't take a drink, he was a fag. Most of the male students took a drink from the bowl however. When they did, they all commented that how good it tasted.

"When do you think that Shaw will be here with his date?" Long asked.

"I don't know. He generally is on time for these things." Galvin responded.

Iota and Sparks looked a bit nervous but they both thought that Shaw would come soon. They both had a bottle of vodka that they were drinking from. What was left they poured into the punch bowl. They were walking in circles around the punch bowl when Shaw came in the room. When they saw him, Sparks said that it was about time that he got there. Iota had a strange look on his face.

"Where's your date?" he asked.

"She's in the ladies room. She'll be here in a minute. What's going on? Don't tell me that you guys put something in the punch bowl. Come on! I'll test it."

He neglected to tell them that he had a bottle of vodka on him as well. He took the ladle and filled one of the glasses that were on the table. He filled it to the brim. He took a sip and said that the vodka was not bad and that it would do. There were other students hanging around the punch bowl. Shaw looked at them, John was there, so were James and some other William, not to be confused with Galvin. They all were horsing around while Shaw remained drinking from the punch bowl. Despite being well dressed in their tuxedos or black suits and dark ties, William, who had been drinking from the punch bowl, grabbed James by the collar of the shirt that he was wearing and pulled at his tie. John began to laugh at the whole episode while Shaw stood there amused at the antics. He finished his drink and then he excused himself.

"I'm going to the men's room. I have to take a leak. That is if you guys don't mind." With that Shaw left all of them standing by the punch bowl, Long, Galvin, Iota and Sparks as well as the other students. Shaw left them and went down the hall to the rest room. Iota said that he needed to go to the men's room too and followed Shaw.

"Wait up, wait for me," he shouted out.

Shaw waited and they both went into the men's room together. They were there for a long time. In the men's room, Shaw was washing his hands at one of the sinks when a shot was fired. The shot made a loud explosive noise. It hit him in the back as he finished drying his hands with the paper towels that were provided for that purpose. He staggered and fell down in the middle of the men's room. He was dead.

"It sure is taking them long," Galvin said.

"It is," Long replied. "Someone should go looking for them. Why don't you go Barry, it sure is taking them a long time. Maybe there's something going on!"

The other students laughed, partly because they suspected that Iota and Shaw were gay. Sparks did not laugh. Long had a reputation for joking around and the other guys expected it, they all laughed at what he had said, all but Barry Sparks. Barry objected when Long told him to go and get them both. He objected whenever Long told him what to do. He complained that he was always asked to do things that he didn't want to do. Long said that he would have gone but he was tired and that Sparks was always whining about something. He preferred to stay where he was, by the punch bowl. While Barry begrudged Steve's order, he nonetheless went down to the restroom. When he opened the door, he saw Shaw lying on the floor with Iota sanding over him.

"My God! What happened!?" He screamed as he ran into the room leaving the door to the restroom open. He knelt beside Shaw who was lying there. He looked up at Iota.

"What happened!? What happened!?"

"I don't know! There was a loud bang from somewhere, from somewhere; and he just toppled over! He just toppled over! I think he's dead! There was a shot! It came from somewhere near the window!" They both looked over at the window but saw nothing.

"O my God! O my God! I'll check him!" Sparks began to shake Shaw. He thought that Shaw might have fainted.

"Wake up! Wake up!" But Shaw did not respond. Shaw turned him over. He had a bullet wound in his back.

The blood began to flow all over the men's room floor. Sparks cried out, a shrill cry that could have been mistaken for the cry of an animal. Somebody had shot Shaw in the back. He looked up again at Iota who was just standing there.

"He was shot! He was shot! You should have been watching him! You should have been watching him! What happened!? Did some guy come in the room!? Was someone else here!? There's a bullet hole in his back! Did some guy have a gun!? I better give him mouth to mouth! Do something, idiot!!"

He was screaming at Iota as he bent over and put his mouth on Shaw's. The other students were now crowded in the restroom. They had all stopped their dancing when they heard the commotion that came from the hallway. The loud music had stifled the sound of the shot that took Shaw's life. The band had stopped playing and they looked at one another and shrugged their shoulders and shook their heads. They had no idea where everybody was running to or why they were running. They had no idea what had just happened in the rest room or why the girls were all screaming.

"What happened?" John said when he got to the door.

"I have no idea," Eric answered. They had gotten to the rest room before the others.

"Why are there girls in the men's room?"

"Let me in, let me in," Long shouted as he pushed his way through the crowd that had gathered there.

He had run to the rest room as soon as he heard the screams coming from there. The girls all looked shocked and had their hands over their mouth while Barry Sparks continued to perform his effort to revive Shaw by giving him mouth-to-mouth.

"Shit! What happened? What happened!?"

Steve Long was visibly shocked at what he was looking at. And it brought back thoughts of a tragedy that he had witnessed just a week ago. He was coming out of a store downtown when an automobile slammed into a group of pedestrians. A man was killed. Three other people were injured. He looked at Iota and then at Sparks who continued to give Shaw mouth-to-mouth resuscitation in the hope of reviving him.

"My God, what happened!?"

Long stood there immobile for what seemed to be forever. Someone suggested that they call the police or at least they call campus security. Long ran out of the room to the phone outside the men's room. He called campus security. They answered with their usual greeting.

"Hello, campus security," the voice said. Long presumed that it was the office secretary.

"Something happened! Something happened! Get someone over here now!"

"Who is this please? Where are you located and what has happened?" She was speaking in a very calm voice.

"Look, get someone over here! Goddamn it! A student was shot! Get someone!"

"Ok, ok, take it easy. I'll have someone there as soon as possible. Where are you located? Should I call the police?"

"Fine, fine, just get someone here immediately! Now! We're at the gym! At the men's room! Call the cops!? Sure!"

When he slammed the phone down, he raced back into the restroom. All the students were standing around the body. They all had a look of horror on their faces. Iota particularly looked strange. Long had a passing thought that Iota looked awful but he focused more on the body. The rest of the students stood motionless. They didn't say a word, but Long knew that they felt awful about what had happened. But what did happen? Long knew that Shaw and Iota had gone to the men's room and that he had sent Sparks after them. He knew that Iota was strange and that Bob Shaw didn't like him very much. Iota had a habit of complaining about everything even more than Sparks did. Iota even complained when they sprayed water in Pierce's office. He didn't like it when Shaw told him to go outside and turn on the water. Long had these thoughts racing through his mind when campus security arrived.

"What's goin' on?" The security officers were dumbfounded at the crowd of students. The students made a lane for them to get through.

"Holy God! What happened here? Is that guy dead?"

"Yeah, I'm afraid so," Iota replied "I think I'm gonna' puke!"

"What happened?" the tall security guard asked.

"Somebody shot him! Don't you see?" Long was getting angry that the security officers weren't doing anything. He said that they should call the local police department. He said that he should have done this in the first place.

"We should call the cops! They'll know what to do!"

Long ran outside to the phone again. He got a dial tone and called 911. When the person on the other end answered, he said that he was a student at Savan and that somebody was shot.

"Could you send someone over!?"

"Where are you located, sir?"

"Goddammit, I'm at Savan College, at the gym, in the men's restroom, on the first floor. Could you please get someone to come!? Please! Someone's been shot I say! Someone's been shot! Where is everybody!?"

He left the telephone dangling as he ran away from it. He looked around for someone in authority. He was looking for Dr. Lane, the Dean of Discipline. He felt sure that he would be there. He felt sure that Lane would call Shaw's parents and he would make sure that there were grief counselors in the morning. He was sure of that. But right now, he only wanted to find him.

"There you are. Where have you been!? Someone has been shot! Don't you see the crowd here? Where have you been!? Were where you!?"

"I was at the dance with the other faculty people."

"Shaw has been shot! Right here in the men's room! He was shot, man, he was shot!!"

"Oh my God! Oh my God! Don't kid me!"

"I'm not kidding! Where have you been!? Good lord, don't you realize that Shaw is dead!? He's dead, dead, dead!?"

"Try to be calm. Try to be calm. I'll call the Dean and lockdown the campus!"

While they were shouting at one another, many of the girls called their parents to tell them about the shooting and that they were alright. They called because it was a part of the drill that they all had participated in when the college first looked at how they should respond if an emergency like the one that just occurred in campus. The shooting of Shaw was certainly an emergency and it fitted into need to call their parents. The girls were highly emotional when they called.

"Hey mother, there has been a shooting here at Savan. Some guy is dead. I'm fine, I'm fine. Please come and get me," one of the girls said while she wept as she spoke to her mother,

She used her cell phone.

CHAPTER EIGHT

The police responded to the call that they received from the 911 operator. Initially they weren't terribly concerned because they had received crank calls from Savan College students before and responded only to find out that it was a prank that the students thought was amusing. On one occasion, someone had called saying that a male student had committed suicide by hanging himself. They rushed to the place at Savan that the student had told them to go to only to find out that it was not true. Nobody had attempted or had committed suicide. On another occasion they received a call from a student that said that some other student had a gun and had threatened to shoot one of the professors. The student that called gave the location at Savan. He said that he would meet the police on the first floor of the administration building when they came and would take them to the classroom where the student had the gun. When the police arrived at the spot where the student had said that he would meet them, they found no one. They proceeded to go to the administration and asked the Dean of Savan whether he had had any complaints recently of someone carrying a gun to class. The Dean immediately suspended classes for the day and locked down all the buildings on campus. The police then went through all of the buildings on campus, interviewing as many students as they could to determine if anyone had a gun or saw someone with a gun. When they had spent the entire day looking for either the gun or the student who made the call, and they were satisfied that neither could be found, they left and went back to the police department headquarters. So they did not take the call that they had received from the 911 operator that someone was shot at Savan too seriously. They kidded around that they had received another call from Savan.

"Hey Clyde, do you want to take this," the Captain asked detective Clyde Longquist.

"Why don't you ask someone else?"

"Hey look, I'm giving you a direct order! Get your ass over to Savan and see what is going on! Take the usual guys with you!"

"Yes sir," Clyde said sarcastically as he leaped out of the chair that he was sitting on and put his cap back on.

The cap once belonged to his father who was a detective on the force three years ago. He had been killed in an armed robbery attempt and, before his death, had made his son promise to wear the cap whenever he did any kind of police work. The cap was much older now and it had been in the family for a long time before Clyde's father had begun to wear it. The police in his department began to call him "Cappy" when he did and that name stuck to him until he died. Clyde had followed his dying wish and wore the cap faithfully whenever he was called out to do any kind of police work. The men kept the tradition alive by calling him "Cappy" too.

"Get your ass in gear, we're going to Savan," he said to the two men who had been assigned to him.

"Yes sir, Cappy."

With that, they left the station. Before they left however, one of the men stopped at the front desk. He told the sergeant who was in sitting there and who was in charge of new cases where they were going and that they would be taking two cars. With that accomplished, they got into their cars and left for Savan College. One of the cars almost hit a pedestrian as they drove down Commonwealth Avenue. They turned when they got to the hill where Savan was located. When they got to the gymnasium and to the first floor where the men's rest room is located, they stopped and got out of their cars. They waited until Cappy got out of his car.

Cappy was in command and he was to lead the investigation in the murder of the student. The police entered the gymnasium and went directly to the men's room. When they got there, Cappy saw the body and all the students standing around. He first put on the white rubber gloves that were mandated by the crime commission. In the past the police who were investigating a crime, were not obliged by the commission to wear rubber gloves and, as a result, they contaminated the crime scene that they were charged to investigate. Cappy didn't want this to happen with this crime scene or with any crime for that matter and he quite willingly put on the rubber gloves. As a matter of fact, he did not even think about it.

He spoke first to Long and asked him what had happened. Long pointed to Iota and told Cappy that he had sent Sparks to the men's room to get both Iota and Shaw, the dead student. Long was quite emotional when he said this. He was still shaken up. Cappy told him not to cry when he noticed that Long was on the verge of tears, that it was not his fault and that it could have happened to anyone. Anybody could have gone to the men's room and put himself in the same kind of danger.

Cappy looked around the men's room while talking to Long. He noticed that a window was opened and told one of his men to go outside and look around. He looked at the body and looked at the wound in Shaw's back. He thought that it was not unusual for a victim to die from such a wound and continued his search and investigation. He noticed that the victim of the crime was wearing a shirt, tie and suit coat. He noticed that Long was dressed in similar style as well. After inquiring why they were both dressed that way, not like the clothing that college students wore to class with the jeans and t-shirt craze that had been defined as the style with some of the student population at Savan, he began to search into Shaw's pockets. They answered his question about how students dressed. They were dressed this way because of the dance. Further they maintained that the dress code at Savan was very strict and it did demand that students were properly dressed when they came to class.

"Look what I found, an earring," he said to himself as he continued to search Shaw's pockets.

While he was searching in Shaw's other pockets, the police officer was outside looking around as Cappy had ordered him. It was dark outside as the September sun silently set over Savan. The police officer saw something glistening on the cool ground. He went over to the spot where he had noticed the object and saw that it was a gun. He exclaimed to himself that this must have been the gun that was used in the murder. He saw that the window to the men's room was opened and that the murderer could have easily shot the victim through it. Without touching the gun [he had learned to not touch anything in a crime scene while in police school], he continued to look around for any other evidence. He had been a good student at the police school. He wore his white rubber gloves with the authority of a man who was possessed with his position.

He went back to the gun and taking a pencil from his pocket, picked the gun up by placing the pencil into its barrel. After looking at the gun more intensely, he decided that he had better take the gun inside and give it to Cappy. He drew a circle where the gun was with a branch of a tree that he found and a piece of chalk that he had in his pocket. He placed the gun gently in a plastic bag that he fished out of another pocket, and he took it into Cappy.

Cappy was continuing his investigation. After finding the earring, he continued searching for more evidence. He ordered the police photographer that had come with him when he first arrived to take pictures of the crime scene. He looked at both Sparks and Iota and began to question them. He asked them what their relationship with Shaw was. When both fumbled with their responses, he became suspicious.

"Could I ask you what your relation with the deceased was?"

"Steve Long was his roommate. Why not ask him?" Sparks appeared to be very nervous when he responded to Cappy's question. Iota remained silent.

"I will. I intend to question everybody that the deceased knew. Let me have your names."

When Iota gave his name, Sparks began to walk out the men's room door. Cappy stopped him and asked him again what his name was. He responded to the request that Cappy made by saying that his name was Barry Sparks and he said to Cappy that he was told by Steve Long to go to the men's room and find both Shaw and Iota. When he said that Cappy should talk to Long about the shooting, Cappy agreed with him and said that Sparks shouldn't worry, that he was going to talk to everyone that knew or came into contact with Shaw. He then turned his attention to Steve Long.

After he had talked to the three students who apparently had a special relationship with Shaw, Cappy told his men to make sure that everything was photographed and not to leave anything out. He also looked around the room with a great deal of intensity. He got a pocket knife from his coat pocket and looked at the body again. He was interested in the slug that took Shaw's life and was intent on digging it out of Shaw's back. His men told him that the coroner would take care of this and he put the knife back in his pocket.

He was looking for any evidence at all that might be useful other than the earring that he had found in the deceased student's pocket. But he found nothing.

His thinking went back to his days at the police academy where he learned about means, motive and opportunity. Surely, the opportunity was there in the men's room. Obviously, the gun was the means; but what about the motive? Surely, Shaw was not liked by everyone. Somebody must have had a grudge against him.

He thought of the three aspects of a crime, means, motive and opportunity. They would all be necessary if a culprit was ever to be brought to justice. All three would be needed if a prosecutor was to convince a jury of guilt in a trial.

CHAPTER NINE

Cappy left the men's room and pushed his way through the crowd that had grown larger. He thought that the crowd would filter out but it hadn't. When he finally was able to get through the crowd, he decided that he had enough of police work and the murder that had happened, and his thoughts wandered to his home life. He thought of his wife, Patricia and his two young daughters Kasie and Calie. He got into one of the police cars and drove home. He thought it was late enough. It was 9pm.

Cappy was a big man. He stood over six feet and weighed about two hundred and fifty pounds. He delighted in working out in the police gymnasium five days every week. He would never miss the workouts if at all possible. He loved the weights, the stationary bicycle and the cross bars. When he was working out, he lifted the weights and rode the stationery bike and all his men looked up to him. They could have been motivated by schadenfreude, but the men watching him workout were only motivated to be like him. They all wanted to be like him. They all had great respect for Cappy. Not only respect, but also they really liked him.

Cappy drove through the heavy traffic in Boston. Much like other drivers in Boston, he occasionally cursed other drivers before coming to his home in Charlestown. He lived in a house that was near the Monument, on Monument Avenue. He parked the police car and went into his home. He was greeted by his wife, Patricia, and his two daughters, Kasie and Calie.

His daughters were twins. He hugged his wife and both daughters and gave them each a gentle kiss on the check. He got out of the police clothing that he had been wearing all day and put on his favorite jeans and t-shirt. He went into the dining room were Patricia had prepared her usual delicious meal, even though it was a lot later than they usually eat together as a family. He sat at one end of the table while Pat sat at the other end.

He delighted in his two daughters, he was very proud of both of them. He asked them both how they did in school and what they had learned. He was aware of the last time that he had gone to the school on parent's night and that the teachers had told him to take an interest in what both of his daughters were doing in school. They were both in high school and Cappy tried very hard to be a good father.

Kasie told him that she had done well in school and hoped that her father would recognize what she had accomplished. She showed him an exam that was returned by one of her teachers. The exam had been graded A by her teacher and the teacher had written on the bottom of her paper a note that praised her effort. She was very proud of this. She had already shown the paper with the note to her mother Pat and to her sister Calie.

"I did well in class today, at least, I thought I did very well," she said as she showed Cappy the paper.

"Sure you did. I'm very proud of you. Very proud," Cappy replied as he studied the paper and the note that the teacher had written.

"Thanks, I promise you that I will continue to do well in school. Hey Calie, wouldn't you just love to be just like me?" She loved teasing her sister.

Calie said nothing. It is not unusual for sibling rivalry to exist in families whether they are twins or not.

Cappy told her that Kasie shouldn't say such things to her sister. Now was the time to eat. After Cappy had said grace, Pat, sitting at the other end of the table, said that she also approved of what Cappy had said. She said that she was really proud of Kasie and the work that she did in school, but she should not have said what she said to her sister.

Cappy hadn't told them about the shooting that happened at Savan yet. In addition to defining the supper hour as the only time that he had with the kids and his wife, he wanted to tell Pat in private. Maybe he was wrong, but this is how he felt.

"I certainly go along with what your father just said." Pat said as she raised her fork from her plate. Pat had thoughts of her own days as a high school student in Philadelphia where she came from. She didn't want to be like her own mother who never took an interest in what she accomplished in school. Pat was always a good student.

They finished eating and took their plates over to the sink. Kasie and Calie had the family responsibilities of cleaning up after they had eaten. They teased one another over the paper that Kasie had shown to her father but that didn't mean that their responsibilities had ended. After dumping the uneaten food into the sink and starting the garbage disposal, they placed the dishes in the dishwasher that was beside the kitchen table. Then they went into the living room to watch their favorite television programs. When they were tired, the children said goodnight and they went to their rooms for their evening rest.

Cappy and Pat were very happy as a couple. They were the envy of the neighborhood, as a matter of fact. This was especially true after Pat had the twins. People often are envious when they see something that they wished happened to them. They frequently gossip about the people whom they envy.

When they went to bed for the night, Cappy still had thoughts of the crime in the restroom of Savan College. Naturally, he could not get it out of his mind.

He frowned as he thought about the many suspects of this crime. He was especially focused on Sparks and Iota. But he was not omitting anybody as suspects. Then he thought about the earring in Shaw's pocket that he had found.

Pat, knowing by the expression on his face, that something was wrong, asked him what bothered him. He hesitated, knowing how upset she would be when he told her what he was thinking about. He knew her personality and the fact that what had happened would be all over the news on television. He knew that he had to tell her. But he thought that he would tell her later when they went to bed.

He turned to his wife after they had gone to bed, but then he hesitated in telling her about the murder at Savan. He was still thinking about the crime and also about the suspects. But he knew that sooner or later she would find out about it and he had an obligation as her husband to tell her.

He turned over from his comfortable position and faced her.

"Are you awake?" He was wide awake when he asked her this question.

"Yes, I am."

"I have something to tell you."

"Yeah, go ahead."

"There was a shooting at Savan today. It was a murder. I was called to the scene of the crime but do not know yet who the murderer is." He said this glumly and he waited for her response.

"My God! A murder! You're kidding me! A murder! My God, what is this world coming to? A murder! Right at Savan College!? You've got to be kidding!" She exclaimed this with a heavy cry as she sat up in the bed.

"Yeah, that's right. A murder! I think that they locked down the campus! They called grief counselors to come in and speak to the students tomorrow. I was thinking about telling you earlier at dinner, but I thought that with the kids around and it was so late when we ate, I really was going to," he yawned. "But now, I really can't sleep. I really can't." Cappy wished that he could.

"Ok, a murder at Savan! I can't believe it! But you need your sleep. Especially tonight if you are going to solve the crime or, at least, be working on it! My poor darling. You work so hard. Try to sleep; try dear. It's silly for both of us to be awake. You need your sleep if you're going to get the one or those who were responsible for such a horrible crime! A murder! I can't believe it! Please! Get some sleep! Please, dear get some sleep."

"Ok, I'll try." He turned over and finally, after tossing and turning in the bed for a while, fell fast asleep.

He got up the next day feeling better. His thinking was still focused though on the murder that had been committed at Savan. He shaved and took care of his morning needs and went downstairs.

His wife had already poured him his morning coffee. He drank it down and said that he didn't want anything else for breakfast. He kissed his wife goodbye and said that he had to get to work. His daughters had already left for school. Pat told him that everything would be alright, that he shouldn't worry. He smiled at her and gave her a long kiss.

He went outside and got into his car. He began the treacherous drive from his home in Charlestown to his office in the Back Bay.

He cursed at the Boston drivers as he drove. He went over the bridge still cursing at them. He kept thinking about the suspects Spark, Iota and Long. But he didn't omit others from his thinking. And his thoughts kept floating back to the earring that he found in Shaw's pocket. He wondered why Shaw would be carrying an earring in his pocket. Did he own it? If it was not his, then who was its owner?

When a car suddenly stopped in front of him, he jammed on his brakes and swore at the driver. He had a heavy foot, but then he wondered whether the man was at fault. Was his thinking about things that he should not be thinking about when he was driving to blame? The cars didn't collide, but the possibility of an accident brought back what his driver's instructor he had years ago had told him. The instructor had told him to always concentrate on where he was going and what he was doing when he was driving, nothing else. Nothing!

The fresh air that he had inhaled when he got out of the car to check if there was any damage had totally woken him up. He thought that maybe he was responsible. He thought that maybe he was responsible because of his thinking about the crime, his swearing at other drivers, and the thoughts that he had about the murder and the suspects to it. He offered the other driver his insurance number but the other driver refused saying that there was no damage done. They both got into their cars and drove off.

When Cappy pulled up to his office, he went immediately to his desk. He didn't bother with the jokes and the humor of the other men. He thought only about the crime at Savan. Pulling out his top drawer, he finally spoke to the other men.

"Has anybody seen my pen and pencil set?"

The other men looked at one another quizzically before answering that they had not seen his pen set; they all thought that Cappy was acting strangely. But when Cappy got up from his chair to leave for Savan, they shrugged and left with him. Cappy told his men to get into their cars and follow him in his.

"Should we have our lights on or the sirens?"

"No, just follow me."

"Ok," they replied.

Cappy was indeed acting strangely they thought. Usually he liked to have them use their lights and sirens when they were going back to a crime scene. They thought that he had changed; this must be more serious than they had thought.

CHAPTER TEN

While Cappy was involved in thinking about his investigation, Pierce was in his office preparing his next class. The books that had been soaked were now dry. He was seated in front of his computer. He typed in the date and the name of the class but then wondered what he should type in next. He just sat there. His mind began to roam with a number of ideas. When he decided on some, he began to type on his computer. He was pleased with the ideas that he had. The ideas rolled of his mind and went directly to the computer screen.

The first thought that he had was to tell the class about the difference between Republicans and Democrats. Students were always arguing about politics but he wondered if they knew what they were arguing about. He typed in the word Democrat and then he typed in the definition of what a Democrat was. He did the same thing with the word Republican. To his way of thinking, the Democratic philosophy was the belief that they had in a strong federal government while the Republican belief was in the notion of freedom of the individual and in capitalism as an economic system. Republicans vary about such things as personal morality and virtue and their religion.

Next, he thought that the students in his class should take an interest in the difference between what was secular and what was sacred. If someone committed a violation of a law that was devised by the agency involved, it would be in the category of being secular and would be considered a crime or a tort. But if someone committed an act that was a violation of a sacred norm, it would be a sin either mortal or venial depending on its severity. He felt that students should know the difference between these two. Very often, he thought, arguments between students who did not know the difference between both of these definitions and their lack of knowledge of this difference was really the cause of their argument. If they had known the difference, they probably would not have argued the way that students often do.

This led him to think about the problem of charisma. Charisma is found in a person's personality when they are able to get people to follow them as specifically a result of their personality. There were many charismatic people in history, Jesus Christ, Martin Luther King,

Gandhi and others who had this gift. The trouble was that structures were necessary in order to maintain and to continue the charisma in succeeding generations that followed the charismatic message. He felt that this was clearly seen in the papacy. In order to maintain the message of Christ to essentially love all people as Christ did, it was necessary to begin a church that was formulated to maintain this message; to have a structure and leadership that set up the rules that were consistent with His message. The papacy, and the structure of the Catholic Church were the natural consequences of this message, and the various buildings and churches were the means that were needed in order to maintain the charisma that Christ had. Pierce was pleased with the thoughts that he had as he continued to type the outline for his class. When he was typing what he thought about the idea of "charisma" he had another thought. This time it was about Max Weber, the German sociologist.

Weber reasoned the same way about charisma and its maintenance. He developed the idea of the "routinization of charisma." By this, he meant the same thoughts that Pierce was thinking about, that in order to continue a message, it had to become routine in the way that people thought. Pierce eagerly continued his typing. He had promised his class, on the first day that he had met with them that he would pass out an outline to them for every class they had and that he would include the assignment for the next class. He would also have a word of the day for them and an expression from some famous person.

The assignment was not a problem for him. The next hundred pages in the text would seem sufficient. But he was stuck on the word and the expression that he would use for the class. After pausing in his typing for a moment, he came up with a word that he thought would help break the ice after what had happened in his office. The word was one the longest one in the English language, "pneumonoultramicroscopicsilicovolcanokoniosis." He could not use the longest word, a word that meant some technical name for Titin which had 189,819 letters to it. He typed the word "pneumonoultramicroscopicsilicovolcanokoniosis "as a part of his outline. After thinking for a while, he thought that he might be arrogant or "showoffy" in using this word. It meant black lung disease or getting silicone in your lungs, but it was not a word that was used often.

Next he had to come up with an expression that he would put on the sheet. The expression that he would use was from Rick Warren's small book, The Purpose Driven Life. "Temptations keep us dependent upon God."

When he finished the typing of the outline, he went up the stairs that led him to the faculty secretary's office. He wanted to make thirty copies of the outline that he had just finished typing. But he saw that somebody else was already using the copy machine. He thought that the person also was a new teacher at the College and that he should introduce himself. He went over to the machine and put his hand out to be shaken. When the other fellow saw him come over and offer his hand, he immediately stopped what he was doing.

"My name is Jeff Fahey. I'm new in the English Department."

"I'm Arthur Pierce in the Sociology Department. I'm new too. Glad to meet you." He shook Fahey's hand and asked him how long he would be at the machine. When he found out that Fahey would not be very long, he breathed a sigh of relief. His class was to begin in only fifteen minutes and he still had to run off thirty copies of the outline, go back to his office, get his notes and brief case, and then get to class.

When Fahey finished what he was doing, Pierce ran off his copies and ran out of the office. But then, he turned around after thinking about what he was doing, and he thanked both Fahey and the faculty secretary, Rebecca. He continued his run again; he rushed down the stairs to his office, collected his books and notes, took his brief case, and left for his class. It seemed to him that he was always in a rush.

As usual, he ran to class. And as he did, he did not look at the trees as they were illuminated by the late September sun. They were all bursting with color. The colors, a combination of yellows, greens and oranges, blended with one another as he ran to his class only to arrive earlier than most of his students. Some though, were already sitting in their seats as he entered the classroom and put his briefcase, notes and the book that he was using on the desk. He sat down and said that he would be glad when this day was over.

Irene Doherty was there. She was early for every class. He explained his fatigue to her in response to the question that she asked him about his health. When all of his students who were coming took their seats, he took attendance. Everyone was in attendance excepting for Shaw, Iota, Galvin and Sparks.

"I guess we can get along without them. Let's begin. First of all are there any questions that you have?" He paused when he asked this question. There were no hands that went up so he began his lecture.

"Today we are going to give you the definitions of Democrat and Republican. I know that a number of debates occur amongst students about politics. When these debates occur, I know that this difference is important. Sometimes we fail in getting definitions correct and that is really the basis for misunderstandings between people when they do not agree.

"A Democrat believes in the power of the federal government. Regulations are necessary in the opinion of Democrats to insure that the rights and the dignity of the person are both guaranteed. The Republicans believe in the rights of the entrepreneur and individualism. The Republicans believe that the entrepreneur has a right to make a profit because he has taken a risk by investing his own money in the system of capitalism. And capitalism allows the consumer to buy products on the market place and this makes for a better society. Society benefits and so does the individual. The individual, unencumbered by government regulations, is free to make his own decisions. If the health and safety of the individual is mandated by what he calls 'government intrusion', this costs the entrepreneur more money. In order to make a profit, he must then jack up the price of the material or goods that the consumer buys."

"How does advertising fit in?" Miss Doherty asked.

"That's a good question. There is recognition on the part of the entrepreneur that the basic needs of the individual for food, clothing and security can be met by natural means; but anything else will be under the rubric of contrived needs. This is what advertising does. It makes us believe that we need the things that are advertised."

"So advertising is responsible for contrived needs? They are not the basic ones?"

"That's right. You can live on brooks or streams of water, but as the Democrats would say, in order to be healthy the government is needed so that the water might be pure. You need an agency to set up the rules for its use. The same thing is true of safety requirements. That's why we have OSHA. OSHA requirements are needed in order to guarantee the safety of the worker. All of this costs money, and the entrepreneur doesn't like it. He feels that the regulations that cost him money will not make for a good society. The same is true of any regulations that make it possible for a worker to expect that his employer will pay him a just wage, one that is consistent with the expectations of the worker and of the culture where the worker works."

He went on to talk about John F. Kennedy, Gandhi and Martin Luther King and their relationship to charisma and what Weber had said about it and the need to routinize it by the growth of structures. He spoke for about an hour and fifteen minutes which was the length of the class, and then he dismissed everyone. As he collected his notes and the books that he used, Bill Galvin and Barry Sparks came into the room.

"How very nice to see you guys. I do hope that I didn't disturb you by my lecture. You were marked absent you know. Where are the other two guys, Iota and your buddy Robert Shaw?"

"Shaw's dead. He was murdered last night. He won't be coming."

"Quit kidding me. Haven't you guys done enough already?"

"We aren't kidding. He was murdered last night."

They all had a very serious look on their faces. Pierce looked at them with a jaundiced eye. He thought that they were the ones, together with Shaw and Iota, who were responsible for the damage done to his office. He knew that Shaw had been their leader and thought that Iota had been involved too. But to say that Shaw was murdered! That was too much!

"You're not kidding me. He was murdered last night!? How did it happen?" He was befuddled with the news. He didn't know how to respond.

"Well, last night, he was supposed to pick up this girl and take her to the dance that was there in the gym. The dance began at six o'clock. But he came alone. When he excused himself to go to the rest room with Iota, they took a long time, so I was sent to find out what was keeping them. I found Shaw lying on the floor. He was shot in the back. He was dead. Iota was just standing there." Sparks did all the talking. He looked very serious.

"My God! I hope you guys aren't trying to kid me."

"We're not. He's dead. We wouldn't kid about something like that."

Pierce was dumbfounded. He didn't like Shaw at all and he knew that he was probably involved in doing the damage to his office, but for him to be murdered! That was too much. He couldn't believe it. He asked Galvin and Sparks to go into more detail. When they did, he felt sick in his stomach, like he wanted to vomit. They told him that Shaw was murdered in the men's room of the gym. They repeated that they had their dance there and Shaw was supposed to bring Megan to the dance. When they finished their story they left the room with their heads hanging. Pierce just stood there. He couldn't move.

"I can't believe it! Right in our own gymnasium! It doesn't make any sense at all! I know that he was not liked by a lot of people, including me, but to murder him! That's preposterous! It doesn't make any sense," he repeated. Then he went back to his office.

Outside, the leaves where turning colors, mostly red and yellow, as they collaborated with the sun's rays. Days were getting shorter and it turned dark around six o'clock. Pierce could think of nothing else but Shaw's murder. When he went into his office, after looking at his books that were partially ruined by someone's idea of a prank or a bad joke, he went over to his desk and sat down. Tears were beginning to swell up in him and he felt this awful sense of failure that he had not done the work that was required of a professor on the college level. In the classroom he should have been more observant. He should have recognized that Shaw was an unusual case, and he should have helped him rather than to tell him that the class was not a gut.

"I should have done more! I should have done more," he kept repeating.

Just them there was a knock on his door. He slowly got up from his chair and wiped his eyes. He went to the door and opened it. A girl was standing there.

"Hi," she said. "May I come in? My name is Megan Sullivan." She was a lovely girl. She had an earring on her left ear and her hair generously cascaded over the right one. She looked like Veronica Lake, a movie actress, with her hair worn that way.

"Oh, I'm sorry. Please, have a seat," he directed her to the chair that faced his desk. "What can I do for you? You look as though I might be able to help. I'll, of course, do what I can." He was surprised to see her. The thought of Robert Shaw was still fresh in his mind.

"Well, as you know, a boy was killed last night at the dance." Tears were beginning to build up in her eyes and threatened to remove the makeup that she was wearing. She tried to hold them back

"I know. I know. What a dreadful thing to happen to a student or to anybody. To be shot in a men's room! To be shot anywhere! What a tragedy! What a tragedy!"

"It is. So sad," she replied.

"It is. It certainly is sad. It's terrible. But what can I do for you?" He hesitated when he said that.

"Well," she said as she leaned over a bit in her chair, "first off don't mention that I came to talk to you, please. I know how people are. They all gossip. All the students do. Then I don't want you to say anything about what I'm going to tell you." Her voice was getting stronger as she spoke.

"Why would you ask me that? To not tell anyone that you came to see me?"

"I don't know. I just thought that it would be better for me if you said nothing about my coming to see you. You know, I was supposed to go to the dance with him; but I stood him up. Please don't say anything to anyone about my standing him up," she said shyly.

"I didn't know that. That's all well and good. I guess that you had your reasons for not going. But you know I can't lie or hold back the truth. If somebody asks me something, I tell them what they want to know. I always tell the truth. I always do. I can't do what you are asking of me. When I am asked a question by the police, or anybody for that matter, I have to tell them what I know. I have to tell them the truth."

"Please. Please? Don't say anything to anybody."

"I simply can't. It is against everything that I have always believed in. I always tell the truth or, at least, I try to." He paused, waiting for a reply. When she said nothing, he continued.

"So you were his date?"

"Yes, I was."

"But you didn't go?"

"That's right."

"May I ask you why?"

"I don't know; I just didn't feel like it. Who knows? You know how it is."

They talked for a little while longer before Megan said that she had another appointment that she had to go to. She excused herself and left the office. Pierce remained at his seat behind his desk deep in thought. He thought about Shaw and what he had said to him the very first day of class. Pierce had words with him in class, and he probably was one of the students who had sprayed water all over his office. He also thought about the visit by Megan and what she asked of him. Of course, the thought of Shaw being murdered haunted him, and haunted all of his thinking. He looked out the window where the students were walking to their classes. The late September sun shone through the trees that were outside the building that his office was in; the sun played with the leaves that were turning to colors of red and yellow. It danced though the trees and suddenly it left; clouds moved in to cover its rays that just a moment ago had been nature's showy pride. He thought that it was the price of living in New England. He agreed with the sage who had said to wait a minute if you want the weather to change. New England weather is always so unpredictable.

CHAPTER ELEVEN

Pierce decided that he would go home to his small three room apartment on Beacon Street. The September sun was getting lower in the sky as the clouds attempted to hide it. He got into his car in the lower parking lot and headed home. His apartment was very small, but he had decorated it as well as could be expected. He had paintings on the wall in his sitting room. A small but efficient refrigerator, a table where he had his meals and a stove where he cooked them graced his kitchen. A sofa together with another chair with a table at either end was in his sitting room. There were bookcases filled with books throughout the apartment, a small television set with a radio and a clock was in the sitting room; and there were knick knacks that offered him memories of his childhood in Charlestown. He took a beer from the refrigerator, put on the television and sat down on the sofa. There was a story on the news that he was watching about the murder at Savan. He watched the news program with intense interest. It was suggested that the murder, which was committed in a men's room at Savan, was committed by someone at Savan. He thought that this was obvious, and that the suspect or suspects should have been identified by now. He was still bitter at the ones who were responsible for spraying water all over his office and destroying the books that he had there. But to think of the murder of a student was another issue! When the news was over and he had finished his beer, he picked up the phone that was sitting on the small table beside the sofa and called for a pizza to be delivered. The pizza was delivered within an hour. He paid for the pizza and gave a tip to the delivery man.

While eating the pizza, he thought that maybe he should talk with Sparks, Iota, Long and Galvin about what had happened. Why was Shaw murdered? Did he have any enemies? Did he have any? Should he have been so harsh to Shaw by sending him to the Dean of Discipline's office? Did he do the right thing? These and other thoughts kept plaguing his mind.

He got another beer from the refrigerator. He took the beer together with the unfinished pizza into his bedroom and began to prepare his class for the next day. As he was doing this, he heard a knock on his door. Immediately, he got up from the sofa and going to the door, he asked who was there.

"Who's there?"

"My name is Detective Longquist. I'm with the Boston police department."

He opened the door and let Cappy in. Cappy took off his coat and cap and, after Pierce had invited him, he took the chair beside the sofa and sat down. Pierce sat down on the sofa. After they exchanged pleasantries, Pierce offered him a slice of pizza and a beer. Cappy, trying to be polite, took the beer and pizza and told Pierce what the purpose of his visit was.

"So, may I ask you what the purpose of your visit is?" Pierce felt obliged to ask this question.

"Sure. I came to discuss the murder of Robert Shaw. I understand that he was one of your students? I also understand that you had difficulties with him? I hear rumors that you thought that he was responsible for the damage that was done to your office at Savan. That's a shame," he paused and consumed the pizza that Pierce gave him and took a long drink of his beer.

"I also hear that you had sent him to the office of the Dean of Discipline. Are these things all true?"

"Yes they are." "I also hear that Galvin, Iota and Sparks were in your class too, along with Shaw. Steve Long, from what I hear, was in another class. Is that right?"

"Yes it is."

"Do you mind if I spoke with all of them?"

"No I don't."

Cappy thought that Pierce was a very agreeable young man. He should interview all of his students he thought. He should interview them all if they were all as polite as Pierce was. He thought that Pierce was very polite but that could be a cover-up if he was guilty of the crime. He would talk to Galvin, Iota, Long and Sparks at the very least and he would also talk with the Dean of Discipline. He thought that there may be others, but talking to them would be a good starting point and talking to all of Pierce's students at Savan might not be easy since he would have to get all of their schedules and it would be so time consuming. After asking Pierce a few more questions about where he was when Shaw was killed, Cappy took his coat and cap from the hook where Pierce had placed them and said his goodbyes.

When he left Pierce's residence, he thought that he would head back to Savan and take another look at the crime scene. He got into his car and went to the College. He got there just as the sun was setting in the West and he went immediately to the men's room in the gym. By the time he got there, it was dark outside. He wished that the summer months would stay around a bit longer than they do because of the length of daylight hours. It was always bright out during the summer months.

He looked around the crime scene after lifting the police tape outside of the men's room. He was glad that his men had remembered to put the police tape up. He was a very meticulous man; he was very proud that this was one of his good characteristics. He had the same expectations of the men who worked for him as he had for himself. His men were aware of this. The tape forbade anyone, other than officials, from entering the location were the crime had been committed.

While looking around the crime scene, which included a chalk drawing of the place where the body was found and the still open window, an autopsy was already underway in the police laboratory. He thought about the autopsy and said to himself that he was a lucky police officer to have all of the necessary equipment and men who were dedicated to their work. Some police departments throughout the country were not as lucky he thought.

He finished looking around and thought of the gun that he had been given and he wondered if the bullet that was going to be extracted in the police lab would be a match. Was it fired from the same gun? His thoughts also brought him back to the earring that he found in Shaw's pocket when he searched through them. He had turned the earring into the police laboratory when they brought the body in. He had hoped that the owner of the earring would be found, but the person was not found yet. After he had finished, he left the men's room.

He thought that he should head home.

Pat was waiting anxiously to tell him all about Kasie's and Calie's day. Calie was doing her homework while Kasie was on the phone but she hung up when she saw her father. Pat was busy in the kitchen preparing the meal for Cappy and the girls. She thought that it would be a good idea to have spaghetti for dinner. She was an excellent cook and her spaghetti was always a hit at home with Cappy and the girls. When he got home, he told her about what had happened during the day. He expressed all of his concerns about the murder at Savan.

"Is everything alright? Are you sure that everything is ok?"

"All is fine. You worry too much," he responded while taking off his coat and cap.

"I don't worry as much as you do. Let's sit down. The spaghetti is ready and the sauce is almost done. The girls had a good day at school."

"Oh, that's good. That's really good." Cappy was tired.

He and the girls proceeded to sit at the table while Pat brought over the sauce from the oven and then got the spaghetti and brought it over to the table. When she sat down in her usual place, Cappy said grace, and they began to eat

"Well, what happened in school today," Pat asked the two girls.

"Not much." It was a response that too many parents are familiar with when they ask their children the same question

"I would appreciate an answer to the question please," Pat responded. "Well," Calie said "we studied the history of the Civil Rights Movement in America; what it was all about and what happened." She said this as she put more spaghetti in her mouth. "Mr. Coughlin told us that Emmit Till's murder was the principle cause of the movement. I always thought it was Rosa Parks or Martin Luther King. Isn't that right Kasie?"

"Yeah, that's what Mr. Coughlin said. You're always right Calie, yes you are." Kasie was occupied with her mashed potatoes which she was devouring despite responding to the question that Calie had asked.

"Don't be a wise guy, Kasie. Well, whatever was said about the Civil Rights Movement, did you guys have a good day at school?"

Cappy was trying to be involved more with his family. He thought that the murder that had happened at Savan had a dramatic effect on his personality. He thought that he should be more concerned with his family, he really should. Kasie and Calie both said that they had a good day at school but that they were glad it was over.

He was worried about what they might think if he told them about the shooting that had occurred at Saven.

The rest of the evening went smoothly. Kasie and Calie went to bed after doing their homework and watching television for half an hour. Watching television, even though it was only for a half an hour, was a reward that they had been given for doing their homework. Both Cappy and Pat had promised them that they would take them to New Hampshire to see their cousins after the business at Savan was over. But Cappy was worried that it would take a long time for the crime to be solved; the people that he had lined up for interviews in his mind would have to be interviewed; all of them. He knew very little about college life or the schedule that students had. And he wanted to interview the Dean of Discipline.

After he kissed the children goodnight, he watched television for an hour and he decided that he would go to bed himself. After he turned the television set off, he asked Pat if she was finished with the dishes.

"I think I will go to bed. Are you finished up? You should go to bed too," he said to Pat.

"I'll be there in just a minute," Pat replied from the kitchen where she was busy washing the floor after she had finished with the dishes. She was always working. She finished washing the floor then she took the mop and pail to the basement. She washed her hands and went to the bedroom. Cappy was already asleep. She changed her clothes, put on her pajamas and went to bed.

Cappy slept well and when he woke up in the morning, he felt rested and alert, but he still was thinking about the murder at Savan and the need to interview the people involved. He also thought that he should go to the coroner's office and find out if the bullet had come from the gun that the policeman brought to him. After he shaved and took care of his personal needs, he came downstairs for his breakfast. Pat and the girls were already up. Pat was busy cooking the bacon and eggs while Kasie and Calie were at the table finishing up their homework. Pat brought the bacon and eggs over to them.

"Do you girls want toast?"

"No thanks," Calie said. "Hey Dad, did you sleep well?"

"Yeah, I did. How about you guys?" Cappy kissed them both on the forehead and he turned around and kissed Pat.

"My, my, you're in a good mood this morning," she said.

"Yeah, I am. I got a good night's sleep and am raring to go," he said with a great deal of enthusiasm.

After he had his usual cup of coffee, and refusing the bacon and eggs that Pat had made, he kissed them all goodbye and went to his car and got in. He drove though the traffic in Boston and went to his office. But he knew he was late because of the traffic. When he got there, his men were already assembled and were waiting for him. They were a bit restless because he was late.

"Hey, Cappy what kept you?"

"I didn't realize the time. I guess I am a bit late," he said as he looked at his watch.

"We forgive you this time," Sergeant Ferguson said with a smile on his face.

"Sure, let's get busy. I need to get to the coroner's office. You guys go to Savan and see what you can find out."

With that, his men left the office leaving him to his own devices. He looked over the paper work that was on his desk that had accumulated since the murder at Savan and filled out a number of forms. One form dealt exclusively with the murder. He looked at it intently before signing his name. Then, when he had finished with the forms, he got up from his desk and headed down the hall to the coroner's office. When he got there, he asked the coroner if the bullet matched the gun that was found outside the men's room.

"Did you finish your work?"

"Of course I did. I worked late last night and was just about to call you. The bullet did match the gun. It was the one that was used in the murder. I also found something else. I found marijuana in the victim's body. It looked like he had been smoking it prior to the murder. I also found traces of alcohol. There were no fingerprints on the gun that was used," the coroner said.

"No fingerprints? It doesn't surprise me that you found traces of marijuana and alcohol in the body. They all smoke grass and they all drink at one time or another. All students do. It doesn't matter where they go. At Catholic schools or secular ones, the problem still exists," Cappy replied.

Cappy was more interested in what the coroner had to say about the bullet and gun. He asked him several questions.

"You say for sure that the bullet and the gun match?"

"Yeah, they do."

"And there are no fingerprints."

"None. The guy who shot the gun must have been wearing gloves or he wiped the gun clean."

"You are sure about that?"

"That's what I said. And they match; the bullet and the gun. There's no question about it."

"Is there anything else that I should know?"

"No, I don't think so. If there is something else, I'll call your office."

"Thanks."

He thought about all the interviews he had to do as he left the coroner's office and headed back to his own office. He thought that he should begin with members of the administration before he interviewed the students. He realized that interviewing them would be more difficult than interviewing the administrators because of their schedules. But now, he was interested in interviewing the Dean of Discipline, Mr. Lane. He realized that the Dean had any number of students that he worked with in his job and Cappy didn't want to appear unaware of this. But he felt that the murder of a student would obviously take precedence over anything else, or that it should. He got into his car and drove to Savan. When he got there he immediately went to Mr. Lane's office, the Dean of Discipline.

"Good day. My name is Clyde Longquist. You can call me Cappy. All my men do. May I see the Dean?" He thought the secretary was very attractive.

"He's with a student now. But if it's urgent, I can interrupt. He won't mind at all. You're more important than a student."

"Thanks, but I'll wait," he replied and he sat in a chair that was beside the door.

When the student exited from the Dean's office, he got up and introduced himself to the Dean.

"Glad to meet you," the Dean said. "Come into my office. Students call it 'the inner sanctum'," he laughed. "My first name is Michael. Just call me Mike."

"I'll be sure not to call your office that. But I will call you Mike," Cappy laughed in return.

They both went into the Dean's office and he closed the door before offering Cappy a seat. When they were settled, the Dean began the conversation. He was called "Lane the Famous" sarcastically by the students.

"How can I help you? I assume that you are here because of the murder that occurred the other night. What a tragedy!"

"It is. It certainly is. Where were you when it happened? I have to ask you this question. I generally ask this when I interview anybody. Think nothing of it."

"I understand. I was here in my office. I had a number of things to do. After I finished, I went to the gym where the students had their dance. That's part of this job."

"Did anyone see you?"

"When I left the office? I don't think so. Not that I know of. My secretary went home hours before. After that, I went right to the gym."

"Did you go anyplace else? Other than the gym I mean, were you outside for any reason?"

"Nope, I went straight to the gym from my office."

"I see. Did you have anything at all to do with Shaw?"

"Yes I did. He was sent to my office by Professor Pierce; something about flooding his office and being a wise guy in class. Pierce is one of our new guys you know. He arrived just this year. He's a good guy."

"Well, may I ask what you said to him? To Shaw I mean."

"I just told him to shape up. It was like a rape case, not that we have had any. It comes down to 'he said, she said.' He told me that he would sue the college. And, I don't want the college to be sued of course. He was a real wise guy though. Apparently he sassed Pierce in class. That's why he was sent down to my office. He was not a kid who could be reformed."

"Hmmm. You really feel that way?"

"Yes I do. Too often these students now-a-days know all about these things, the way to speak to anyone in an official capacity. When they get in any kind of trouble, they all say that they are going to sue the College. That's what they say. That's what they use as a defense. They all are problems. I deal with problem students every day."

"I guess you get fed up at times?"

"I sure do."

"That's interesting," Cappy mused.

"Well I wouldn't do anything to them, other than talk to them or expel them from school. That would be the worst punishment I could impose. Now don't think that I had anything to do with Shaw's murder because of what I've said," the Dean was now sweating a bit.

"I'm not thinking that at all. I have to look at all possibilities though." But Cappy did notice the small beads of sweat on the Dean's forehead but said nothing about it.

"Anything else that might be of help? Anything at all?" Cappy was trying to be as complete as he could.

"I don't think so. If I think of something else I'll call your office. Leave your number with my secretary."

With that, the Dean got out of his chair. He was a big man and getting up was not easy for him, but he managed. Cappy also got up from his chair and extended his hand to be shaken. They shook hands and Cappy left the office. Before he left, he gave the Dean's secretary the phone number at his office in the Police Department. After exchanging pleasantries with her, he left the building, got into his car and drove back to the Police Department.

When he got there, he looked exhausted, but he soldiered on. His men were all assembled and waiting for him. They all wanted to go home but not before Cappy gave them his permission. They all thought that they had a long day, going to Savan, investigating the crime scene as much as possible and putting up the tape and closing the rest room door. Just as Cappy gave them his permission for them to go home, the phone rang. It was the coroner. Cappy answered it and after saying hello, he asked him if he had any news that would help him in his investigation. In particular, did the coroner find out who owned the earring and did he identify the slug that had killed Shaw?

"I do. I found traces of DNA on the earring that you left for me to look at. I went through all the files of the Department, but found nothing there. Then I had the bright idea of going through the files at Savan. I did it on-line. When I did, I came up with the name of Megan Sullivan. The slug came from the gun that the policeman found outside."

"You're a good man! Megan Sullivan, huh. I'll have to go see her."

CHAPTER TWELVE

Cappy had all the information from the coroner that he had called for. But he didn't have the information about the gun and the bullet match. When he got the information that he called for, he thanked the coroner and hung up the phone. He left his desk and let his men go home. He thought that they and he had enough for one day. He decided to go home himself.

The sun was setting when he got to his car. It had a glow that lit up the field that was beside his office. It was like someone had put a match to it and it was burning. It appeared like it was on fire, all red and orange. It was like burning coals were all over the field. He looked at it and said to himself that it was certainly a beautiful sight.

"I'm home," he said when he got there.

Pat and the girls had been waiting for him. When he came in the door, they all greeted him with warm words. They asked how his day was and he responded that the day was fine and asked them about theirs. They took turns saying their day was good and both the girls gathered around him, hugging and kissing him. Pat said that her day was fine for her too, and she kissed him on the lips. Cappy was surprised when she did this.

"My, my. That's a pleasant surprise. What's got into you?"

"Well the girls got their report cards today. They both did so well; they made the honor roll! I'm so happy and pleased."

"That's great! Congratulations girls," Cappy responded.

"Now, I can get back to what I was doing," Pat said as she went back into the kitchen. She asked them what they wanted for supper and when they all responded that the lasagna that she made was awesome, she decided that's what she would make.

When they were all seated at the table, Cappy said grace and they began to eat the lasagna that Pat had just cooked and put in front of them.

"It really is good," Kasie said.

"It sure is," Calie replied as she shoved another layer of lasagna into her mouth.

"It is indeed," Cappy chimed in.

The rest of the supper time turned into gossip about their neighbors who had been bothering them. And both girls told Pat and Cappy what went on in school that day. They finished with desert and after Pat took the plates and utensils over to the dish washer with the help of the twins, they all did their usual routine. The girls went into the living room to do their homework while Cappy watched the news on television. The news was on the murder that had occurred at Savan. It gave gruesome details of the murder but focused more on Savan College and the apprehension that parents have about sending their children off to that college or to any college for that matter.

The girls finished up their homework. They went over to Cappy, kissed him on the forehead and went to their bedroom. Cappy said that he was tired too and went to bed.

"I'm going to bed, Pat. I have to get up early in the morning."

"That's fine dear. Sleep well. I have a few more things to do."

With that, she went into the living room and opened the desk drawer. It had bothered her for a long time that it had been sticking and she wanted to fix it. After she did her work on it and complained that she had to do everything, fix everything, she went to bed herself. Cappy was fast asleep when she got to the bedroom. She kissed him on the forehead and got into bed herself. She reached over and set the alarm for early in the morning and snuggled up to Cappy. He moved for a brief second; it was obvious that he was fast asleep. She looked at him lovingly for a moment, went on her side and, before a minute had passed, went to sleep herself.

When the alarm clock went off and the sun peered through the window calling him to another day, Cappy reluctantly got up. He yawned and after doing his morning ablutions, he went downstairs ready to greet his family and another day. He had his morning coffee and almost immediately his thoughts went to Savan and the shooting that took place there. He spoke to himself and said that he had a lot of people to talk to; Sparks, Iota, Galvin, and anybody who witnessed the shooting or had been in the area. He had already spoken to Lane and Pierce. He thought that it would be better, according to his schedule, to interview Megan Sullivan last. The fact that she allowed Shaw to have her erring fascinated him. What reason did she have to allow him to have one earring? Or maybe he just took it. He finished his coffee as the rest of his family were getting up and kissed them goodbye. He went out to his car and drove to his office in the Back Bay part of the City. As he went over the bridge, he thought of the interviews that he had to do. His mind was clear because of the good night's sleep he had during the night, but it was clouded by thoughts of these interviews. By the time he got to his office, that's all he could think of.

"Good morning, sir. I hope you're well today," one of the officers in the outer office inquired.

"I'm fine," he responded gruffly. "How you doin'"

"Good, good," the officer said.

The rest of the men greeted him and he went into his office

"Well, that's over," he said to himself as he sat down at his desk. "Look at all the things I've got to sign!"

He took the pen out of his jacket pocket and signed the sheets. After finishing all the paper work that he had to do, he went from his office to the outer office and gathered his men. He told them to follow his car and they all went to Savan. When he got there with his men following him in their cars, he went immediately to the Academic Dean's office and spoke to the secretary.

"Good morning. Do you have the schedule of these students?" He laid the paper with the names of the students that he wanted to speak to on her desk.

"Just a moment, sir." She got up and went to the filing cabinet.

She got the schedules that Cappy wanted. He thanked her and walked into the hall. There he met the Dean of Discipline, Mr. Lane, who appeared out of nowhere and asked him what he wanted. He said that he was looking for the schedule of the students he wanted to interview. After telling the Dean of Discipline that he got what he was looking for in the Academic Dean's office, they both smiled and Cappy went on his way. He thought that Lane was different from when he spoke to him at the interview. He thought to himself that he should speak to him again; but at least he got the schedules that he wanted. Now he had to interview them. The list included Iota, Sparks, Galvin and Long. He thought that he would talk to Galvin first.

He noticed that Galvin was in Professor Pierce's class along with Sparks and Iota. As a matter of fact both Sparks and Iota roomed with him. Robert Shaw was in the same class, his roommate, Steve Long, had taken another course that was offered at the same time. He would talk with him later on. Finding Galvin was not as difficult as he thought it would be. Having his schedule was a big help. Even though it was still early, around eight thirty in the morning, the students who didn't have a class at that time would still be sleeping, he decided that he would go to Galvin's dorm room and talk to him there assuming that he was still in the room. Cappy thought he might still be in bed as he knocked on the door of Room 220 in Kasper Hall. When somebody shouted out who the person was who was knocking at the door so early in the morning, Cappy identified himself as being with the Boston police. When he said that he was with the Boston Police Department, the door opened quickly. Galvin's roommates, Mark Iota and Barry Sparks were not there. Bill Galvin just stood there half naked. His eyes were half opened.

"Good morning, sir. I didn't know who was knocking."

"Good morning. I'm with the Boston Police. May I come in? I have a few questions that I need to ask you."

"Sure, sure, come on in! Come on in."

"Thanks."

He went into the room and looked around. There were the usual posters on the wall and bookcases that were filled with books and nick-knacks, and a closet that was filled with clothing. There also was a desk, two chairs and two small beds. He sat in one of the chairs and beckoned Galvin to sit in the other one. When Galvin sat down, he began his interview.

"I'm here to talk about the shooting that took place in the men's room of the gym earlier this week."

"I figured."

"Don't be scared. I just have a few questions. Could you tell me where you were when the shooting took place and what you were doing?"

"Sure. I was at the dance, standing near the punch bowl most of the evening. Girls make me nervous and I am generally scared to ask them to dance. Please don't tell anyone. Shaw and Iota went to the head and Long sent Sparks to see what was keeping them. They were gone a long time. That's all I know."

"That's it? You were at the dance and you were just standing around the punch bowl. Is that correct?" Cappy was as inquisitive as he had ever been with his interviews.

"Yeah, that's right."

"Did you hear a shot? Anything unusual?"

"No I didn't. The band was playing loud and all the kids were jumping up and down. I didn't notice anything that was unusual."

"Don't be nervous. You didn't hear a shot? The band was playing too loud?"

"Yeah, they were."

"Whose idea was it to send someone to get Shaw and Iota?"

"It was Steve Long's idea, He sent Sparks. Sparks doesn't like being told what to do, especially by Long."

"Sparks was the one who gave the victim mouth-to-mouth?"

"That's right."

"Do you think that Sparks was the one, the murderer?"

"Nah, I don't think so. He's not the type. You get to know people and what they are all about when you go to college."

"I hear what you're saying."

"Anything else?"

"Nah, I'll be going now. I guess I have all I need. You have nothing else you want to say?"

With that, Cappy got up from his seat and bid adieu to Galvin. Galvin said, "See ya. Goodbye. I might go back to sleep. I had a bad night last night and don't have a class till late in the afternoon."

Cappy left the room got into his car and headed home. He parked near his home on Monument Avenue. He was lucky to find a spot that was free. He thought that most people in Charlestown couldn't tell the difference between Monument Square, Monument Avenue and Monument Street. He shrugged his shoulders heavily when he thought about it and went into his home. He was greeted by his wife and two daughters.

"Hey, sweetheart how was your day," he asked.

"Hi darling. My day was good. How was yours?" She kissed him on the cheek.

"Fine, fine, where are the girls? Oh, here they are," he said teasingly. He picked them up one after another; first Calie then Kasie, and he kissed them both.

"My, my you girls are getting so big! I will soon have trouble picking you guys up. Maybe by next week! What's for supper Pat?"

"Nothing much. I tried something new for tonight. Maybe you'll like it. I don't know. It's corn and chicken mixed, plus, of course, veggies and a salad. It will be ready in twenty minutes. Why don't you relax and put on the news?"

"Ok, I'll do that," he responded.

He went into the parlor and sat down in his favorite chair and put on the television. The news broadcasters were talking about politics and the current congressional elections. Later they switched to the news about the shooting at Savan. When Pat called him to come to the kitchen for supper, he shut off the television and went to the kitchen. He took his usual seat at one end of the table while Pat sat at the other end. The girls sat across from one another.

"What did you girls learn in class today?"

"Nothing much, dad. Mr. O'Toole spoke about his experiences in Ireland," Calie said.

"Yeah, he always talks about Ireland, Dad. I don't know what he says half the time." Kasie was getting a bit fidgety when she talked about her favorite teacher, Mr. Neil O'Toole.

"I always think about Notre Dame when people talk about Ireland and the Irish. I know I am in the minority, but I can't stand it when the people who broadcast their football games on television refer to them as 'The Irish'. I just can't stand it! The only reason they are called 'The Irish' is because some sports writer said that they played football like a bunch of drunken Irishmen. It is a French school! The name of the school, 'Notre Dame', means 'Our Lady', for Pete's sake. It's not an Irish school. Don't get me started! It was formed by the French who came down from Canada and started the school that they called 'L'Ecole de Notre Dame'. Don't get me started.

"Further, Boston College and Holy Cross are the real Irish schools. They were founded in order to protect the Irish Catholics from the mentality that was started by Harvard and Dartmouth colleges. Just read John Donovan's book, The Academic Man. Don't get me started!"

"Dear, you're getting upset. Maybe you shouldn't talk about Notre Dame," Pat replied in her usual calm manner.

"Yeah, I know. But you know how I feel about them. Whenever they play football, or any game for that matter, I always root for the opposing team. That's the kind of guy I am, I guess. But they do irritate me," Cappy said as he finished his meal.

"Do you want dessert?" Pat asked the girls and Cappy. "I'll get some," Pat said as she went to the refrigerator.

"Further, they refer to 'Touchdown Jesus' extending His arms as though he was an official announcing a touchdown. The painting that they have on the library facing the stadium shows this. They are doing a very real disservice to an institution that has made such tremendous progress on an intellectual level. I'm sure that God doesn't care who wins and who loses a game, and it's only a game! Who does He root for when Notre Dame plays BC or Holy Cross? Don't get me started!" He said all of this while smiling.

"Hey dad, don't you think you're going too far? We all love Notre Dame." Calie was just finishing her supper and looked forward to having desert.

"Groovy, I totally agree with Calie, totally," Kasie said.

"Speak English please, don't use words that might make sense to your peers but not to your parents," Pat calmly replied as she went to the refrigerator. She didn't like it nor did she understand words that young people used.

"Let's not talk about it. How's the dessert?" Pat appeared to be anxious.

"It's fine, just fine, 'Great' might be more appropriate," Cappy said. The family all agreed that the dessert was excellent.

Cappy finished and went into the living room while Pat and the girls put the dishes in the washer. When they finished their chores, the girls went to their room and finished up their homework before taking advantage of the half hour that was allotted to them to watch television. Cappy was half asleep sitting in his chair as the girls put the television on with the volume down low so they did not disturb him. When their time was up, they kissed Cappy goodnight on the forehead; they kissed their mother goodnight in the same way and went to bed.

The next day Cappy, feeling refreshed from a good night's sleep, had his usual cup of coffee and, as was his custom, refused anything more when Pat offered him breakfast, gave her and the two girls a kiss goodbye and went off to work. On his way, he thought of the interviews that he needed to do. He thought that he would interview Long, Shaw's roommate today. But what about the owner of the earring . . . Megan Sullivan? Had she given it to him? Did he take it? How? He wasn't quite sure of when he would interview Sullivan.

When he got to his office he was greeted by the captain of detectives and by Sean Muldoon. His captain told him that Muldoon was assigned to him. He was a rookie. Cappy was glad to have Muldoon to talk to as well as teaching him the various "tricks of the trade." Cappy asked his captain whether he was going to eliminate the two men who had been assigned to him. When the captain said no that he was not going to eliminate anybody but that he figured that Muldoon would be well suited to take notes of what Cappy might ask. Cappy said that he was pleased to have Muldoon. He thanked the captain and shook hands with Muldoon.

They left the office and headed for Savan. When they got to the college, Cappy, along with Muldoon, went directly to the Academic Dean's office. They spoke to the secretary and told her that they were going to interview Stephen Long. Cappy told her that because he wanted everything to go as smoothly as possible. Sometimes when people do things without informing all the people involved, people get a bit upset. It is always better to be safe than sorry Cappy reasoned. When they left the Academic Dean's office with heads down, they bumped into the Dean of Discipline who was waiting to see the Academic Dean. Cappy thought that it was curious that Lane was there but he smiled and said hello. He introduced Muldoon to both the Academic Dean and to Lane then he looked at the schedule of the classes that students had at this hour and also where their dormitories were.

The schedule that he had for Long showed that he had a class with Professor Mark Bourque in the afternoon. They went to Room 4 where Bourque had his class and requested from the professor that he speak to

Long. Professor Bourque gave Long permission to leave the class and speak to both of them.

"Hi Steve, my name is Clyde Longquist. I'm with the Boston police. You can call me Cappy. All my men do. This is Sean Muldoon my assistant. He will be taking notes of this meeting, that is if you don't mind."

"Yeah, I remember you. You were the guy who came the night that Shaw was killed. What's this all about anyhow? Hi Mr. Muldoon. How ya doin?"

"It's about the murder," Cappy answered leaving Muldoon simply to record the conversation. Muldoon took out his pen and recorded what Cappy asked him. Muldoon seemed a bit nervous.

"I thought so."

"Could you tell me where you were?"

"I was beside the punch bowl. I was just standing around when Shaw came and said that he was not with his date because she was in the lady's room. He said that he had to go to the men's room and Iota went with him. I sent Barry Sparks to find out what was taking them so long. That's it."

"Did you hear any sound? Did you hear a gun being fired?"

"No, I didn't."

"Was Iota or Shaw carrying a weapon?"

"Hell no. They weren't."

"How do you know?"

"I just do, that's all. They weren't carrying a gun or anything,"

"You're sure about that?"

"Yes I am. I went to the men's room when I realized that something was wrong. I saw Shaw lying there and Iota standing beside the body."

"No kidding. How come you didn't hear anything?"

"I guess the band was playing loud music. I really don't know. But I didn't hear a thing. I just sent Barry Sparks to see what was keeping them."

"Sparks gave him mouth to mouth?"

"Yeah, he did."

"Do you get along with Sparks?"

"No, I don't. Why?"

"I'm just asking. Who was Shaw's date that night? Was it the Sullivan girl? Megan Sullivan?"

"I don't know. Maybe. It could be. Shaw said that she was in the ladies room when he came to the dance. Maybe it was her, I saw her at the bar down the street. She came up to Bob and asked him to take her to the dance."

"She did?"

"Yeah."

"That's unusual for a girl to ask a guy. Is there anything else that you can remember that might help us find the responsible person or persons?"

"Nope, no I don't think so," Long answered as he moved from the wall.

Muldoon jotted all of this down in his small notebook. Cappy told him that he was calling it a day because he was not feeling well. They went back to their car and headed back to the office. After leaving Muldoon there, he went home to Charlestown. He was greeted his wife and told her that he was not feeling well and needed a nap. He went to the bedroom and went to bed and lay down.

He was still thinking about the murder at Savan.

CHAPTER THIRTEEN

Cappy felt better when he woke up the next day. He thought that it must have been something he ate or perhaps the strain of the forensic investigation. At any rate, he felt a great deal better than he had the night before. He was still intent on the interviewing process and thought that he would interview Barry Sparks next. He proceeded to get out of bed, kiss his wife Pat and tell his children goodbye and went to Savan. On the way he stopped and picked up a cup of coffee at one of the coffee houses that he frequented. He sipped it slowly. He felt better after he drank it.

He went to the Academic Dean's office with Muldoon to get Sparks' schedule for that day and again they ran into Lane. Cappy thought it strange, but Lane's office was near the Academic Dean. Frequently, the Dean of Discipline at any college would go to the Academic Dean's office to chat or to seek advice. It should not be a surprise for Cappy to run into him again in the hallway near the Academic Dean's office, but it did bother him some. He thought that it was very unusual to see him again when all he wanted was Sparks' schedule.

"Good morning Mr. Lane. How are things going this morning? You remember Muldoon."

"I do remember him from our prior meeting. How you doin? I'm feeling well. Thanks for asking. How are the twins?"

"They're fine. They're fine. I wasn't feeling very good last night, but I think that it's gone away now, at least I hope it has," Cappy replied while he looked at Sparks' schedule.

"I'm glad you're feeling better. It must be the work that you're doing on the murder. How's it going anyhow?"

"Ok. It's going ok. At least I hope that it's going ok."

"Well, if there's anything I can do, don't hesitate to call my office. I'm glad to help if I can."

Cappy and Muldoon left the hallway outside the Academic Dean's office and went looking for Sparks. Since he did not have a class until the late afternoon Cappy felt that he would still be in his dorm sleeping. Students do love to sleep he thought as he went to Kasper Hall where Sparks lived with Galvin and Iota. He thought for a while and it suddenly dawned on him that Galvin and Iota had lived with Sparks in the same dorm room. The College didn't like to have three students in the same room, but at the present time it was a necessity with so many freshmen applying to Savan. He knocked on the door and Galvin answered.

"Oh hi, it's you guys. Did you want to ask me more questions?"

"No, not this time. I'm looking for Barry Sparks."

"He's still sleeping, but I'll wake him up." He moved over to Sparks' bed avoiding the sleeping Iota as much as possible but to no avail. He bumped into Iota's bed in his effort to wake Sparks up.

"What's going on?" Iota rubbed his eyes as he sat up in his bed. "Oh, it's the detective. He's got somebody with him. Does he want me?"

"No, he wants Sparks this time," Galvin said as he shook Sparks who managed to sleep through all the noise. Muldoon just stood there with his pen and notebook.

"What? What's goin' on?" Sparks rubbed his eyes before looking at Cappy. "Oh, it's you. What do you want?"

"Not much. I just want to talk to you. Would you other guys excuse us?"

"Sure, sure, no problem," Galvin was already dressed. He hustled Iota to put on some clothes. "We'll go to the coffee shop and you can have all day."

Sparks was still blurry eyed. He put on some clothes after he got out of bed. He went to the chair and sat beside Cappy. Muldoon remained standing where he already was ready to take notes of the interview.

"What can I do for you," Sparks said. His eyes were still blurry. He didn't like to be woken up so early in the morning. At least to him it was early even though it was late in the morning. Students do like to sleep in.

"I just want to ask you a few questions. Do you mind?"

"No, I don't," he answered still half asleep.

"First of all, could you tell me where you were the night of the murder? Don't be too concerned. This is a question that I ask everybody who has anything to do with the tragic circumstance of the shooting that occurred the other night."

Muldoon stood by busily taking notes that he recorded in his notebook.

"No problem. I was beside the punch bowl and Steve Long asked me to go to the men's room to see what was taking Shaw and Iota so long. When I got there, Shaw was dead and Iota was just standing there, I gave Shaw mouth to mouth hoping I could get him breathing again. But I was not able. Long came in and called security, I think, and then someone called the cops. You came with them. That's all I know."

"Ok then. Did you hear a gun fire? Anything unusual. Try to think. Anything at all?"

"No, I didn't hear anything unusual. Nobody heard the gunshot. The band was playing and all the kids were dancing and having a good time. All of it is so tragic. He was such a good kid, he really was."

"I understand that you had little use for Steve Long."

"That's right," he paused, "he was always giving orders to everybody. I didn't like it. He gave me orders to go to the men's room that night, or as he would say, 'requested that I go'."

"So let me get this straight. Long told you to go to the men's room and when you got there you saw the body and Iota was standing over it?"

"That's right. That's all I know. I gave him mouth to mouth resuscitation that we learned the first day we had health class. I never thought I would use it though."

"Good. That's about all that I have. Is there anything that you may have overlooked?"

"I don't think so, I got there and saw Shaw, the window was open and Iota was just standing there."

"The window was opened? You didn't mention that."

"I guess I didn't. Is that important?"

"Yes it is. The window is very important. It was level with the place where a person would wash his hands?"

"Yeah, I guess so."

"Well, thanks for your time. I'm sorry I interrupted your sleep. You can go back to bed now."

"Thanks. But now that I'm up, I think I'll stay up and head to the coffee shop. The other guys are there. Right?"

"Yeah, I think so. Thanks for your time," Cappy said as he put his cap back on and left the room. Muldoon followed after him closing his notebook. Cappy thought about the window being open. He thought that it could have been used in the shooting since it faced the sink where Shaw was washing his hands.

They both walked outside and looked at the trees turning colors. Cappy was always amazed at nature and how it seemed to have a mind of its own when seasons change. Of all the seasons of the year, he loved the fall. The trees and their falling leaves blended together in a display of red and yellow. They looked quite lovely to him. It reminded him of a poem that he read when he was younger. It was by Thaddeus Rutkowswki entitled Yardbirds of Vermont. Not everybody understood the poem, but to him it was one of his favorites. It talked about how birds often desecrated trees where they shouldn't be. Trees are much too splendidly beautiful with their magic shift in color from green to red and yellow.

They got back into their car and Cappy had to decide about going back to his office or going home for the day. He admitted to Muldoon that he still was not feeling well, but decided that they had better head back to his office. When they got there, he was glad that he had made the choice that he did. The captain was waiting for him and asked him about the interviews that he had conducted. He asked him how he got along with Muldoon and Cappy answered fine. Also, the captain told him that the coroner had called. Cappy said to the captain that he had spoken to Pierce, Lane, Long, Galvin and Sparks and that he intended to speak with Iota as soon as he could. He also told the captain that he needed to talk to Megan Sullivan. When he gave the captain his report he went over to his desk and picked up the phone. He dialed the coroner's number.

"Hello, you called?"

"Yeah, I did. I wanted to know if you were through with your interviews. Did you speak to Megan Sullivan yet?"

"No, not yet. Why?"

"I just wanted to give you a head's up. She was pretty wasted at the Lamppost the other night when she asked Shaw to go to the formal with her. The invitation was her doing, not his. To top it off she left the bar with another student, Ray Romano."

"Hmmm. How do you know that little piece of information? I'm not sure that it changes things, but thanks, I'm grateful for all that you've done."

"No problem. I can't reveal my source, but let's say that it's highly reliable,"

"It must have been the bartender. He's always mouthing off to someone or another."

"Maybe. But I can't say any more. Make sure that you interview her though."

"I will," Cappy said as he hung up the phone.

Cappy then signed a number of forms that were left on his desk before he went home. Muldoon glared at his watch. It was obvious that he wanted to go home. Cappy kept thinking about what the coroner had told him about Megan and her behavior at the Lamppost. She was only a freshman he thought and, so far as he knew, Romano was a senior. He thought that it was a bit strange for a senior male to be interested in a freshman girl. But it is not unusual. It happens all the time. At least at Savan. Senior males are typically prone to this kind of behavior. He was still not feeling well, but there still was a lot of work for him to do. The forms where still there. He had to read all of them and sign all of them

He was a bit annoyed that he had to print his name beside his signature. He kept thinking about the interviews that he was going to conduct with Iota and the girl. He stayed at his desk signing papers. There was another phone call. He answered it. It was Megan Sullivan.

"Hello, this is detective Cappy Longquist," he answered brusquely.

"Hi, this is Megan Sullivan calling. I heard that you were talking to some of the boys and wondered if I was on your list too. I'm going home to Connecticut in a little while, so if you want to talk to me you need to do it now. I'm in room 201 in Halley Hall."

"Sure, sure that's great. I'll be over shortly."

He finished the forms that were on his desk and he told the captain that he was going back to Savan to interview one of the students. The captain said that it was fine so long as he finished the work that was on his desk and he took Muldoon with him. They both got into a police car and headed for the college. The traffic was still heavy this time of day but Cappy, who was driving, managed to get through it without cursing or swearing at the other drivers the way that he generally did. When they arrived at the college, they looked for Halley Hall. The buildings at Savan were built only recently and they were attractive. When they finally found Halley Hall among all of the dormitories that they had at the College, he looked for Room 201. Cappy knocked on the door.

"Who is it," came the reply from the room.

"It's Cappy Longquist. I'm the one who was on the phone. I'm with the Boston Police and I came to talk to Megan Sullivan."

"Oh, it's you. Just a minute," she said from inside the room. Megan was packing her things so that she could get home to Connecticut. She opened the door for Cappy and Muldoon. They came into her room. Cappy looked around casually and said that she had nice living quarters.

"This is Sean Muldoon, my assistant. He's only here to take notes. You have a nice room here. I'll bet that you will miss it," he couldn't think of anything else to say.

"How do you do Mr. Muldoon? Yeah, it's nice but I can't wait to get home. Especially with all that has happened here. I'm not even sure that I will come back. My roommate, Gabriella LaRocha, is not here. She wants me to return."

"You might have to. But for now we just have a few questions that I'm going to ask you if you don't mind." He further said that Muldoon's function was to take notes.

"No, I don't mind. Anything I can do to help is fine. That's why I called you."

"First of all, did you have anything to drink at the Lamppost the night before the tragedy?"

"Yes I did. I'm not used to drinking any beer and I'm afraid I had too much."

"Did you leave with anybody?"

"Yes I did. I was foolish and I left with a guy by the name of Ray Romano. He tried to get fresh with me. Right here in this room."

"He did something?"

"No, he didn't do anything but he said some awful things."

"Like what? I have two girls, they're twins, and I know how protective you have to be. Did he say anything to you that might have anything to do with the murder of Shaw? Anything at all?"

"No. Nothing like that. But he did suggest that the bed was too small for both of us to fit into, then I asked him to leave, or I told him to. One thing more that I should tell you though. I spoke with Professor Pierce and asked him to not mention my name or anything. I just don't like to get involved. I know I shouldn't have and that's one more reason I called you. My conscience is very frail."

"You probably should not have left with Romano or spoken to Pierce, but that's neither here nor there."

"Thanks. That's why I called. I don't want to leave Savan and have this hang over my head."

"No problem. Now, may I ask you a few questions?" The thought of the earring was still bothering him.

"I'll help in any way I can."

"Good. Could you tell me what happened?"

"Well, when he left, that pig Romano, I was tired and went to bed, by myself of course. But before I did I went down the hall to see Moira and Samantha. They're friends of mine. They were at the bar the night I left with Romano. I told them about my plans to get Shaw. I asked him if he wanted to go to the dance with me. I didn't like him at all. I don't like to talk bad about the dead, but I think I hated him. He was so conceited. He was on the basketball team and was pretty good. He was an All American selection in high school you know. But he was so conceited! I really didn't like him."

"Where Moira and Samantha fans of Shaw? Or was Gabriella?"

"No, they weren't. When I was in the bar with them they all thought it was fun for me to ask Robert to go to the dance with me. Gabriella thought so too. She was not in the room when I got back with Romano. I don't know where she went. She was not a fan of Shaw though; in fact she didn't like him at all. She was not a basketball fan either. She didn't go to any games."

Cappy thought that he would have to interview the girls too, particularly Gabriella, since she was Megan's roommate and the probable leader of the girls. Then he thought about the earring. In the meantime, Muldoon was taking notes as quickly as he could.

"I found an earring in Shaw's pocket. Did it belong to you?"

"My goodness, I have been looking for it. Is it a pearl erring with a diamond in the center?"

"Yeah, that's the one. How did it get into his pocket? Did you give it to him?"

"No, no, do you have it?"

"No I don't. It's in the coroner's office together with the other evidence."

"Evidence? Is my earring a part of that stuff?"

"Yes, I'm afraid it is. Did you give it to him?"

"No I didn't. He must have taken it."

"He came into your room? Why? Weren't you here?"

"No, I wasn't here. He must have knocked on the door and when no one answered he must have come in by himself. He was not invited. No, he wasn't. He must have come in by himself and looked around. Maybe he went to the box where I have my jewelry and took the earring. If he did, he did it all by himself. I didn't tell him to take it."

"But why would he take it?"

"I don't know. I have no idea why he came into the room or why he would have taken the earring. I was going to stand him up that night. I wished that I didn't. I wish I never met him. I really do. But at the time I thought it was funny. So didn't the other kids. But why he decided to come in and take the earring, I have no idea."

"But you don't know for sure that he took the earring?"

"No I don't, but he must have. He had it, didn't he? I didn't give it to him."

"Ok. Ok. Let me summarize. You were in the Lamppost with the girls and you went over to Shaw to ask him to take you to the dance. He said fine then you went back to the table and spoke to the girls who thought it was funny. They left but you stayed behind and went back to the dorm with Romano. Gabriella was not here. He made a move on you and you told him to leave. The next night you were not at the dance. You suspect that Shaw came into your room and took the earring. Is all of this right?"

"Yes it is."

"You would swear to this in court?"

"Don't tell me I have to go to court! That's the last thing I want to do. I really would hate to do that. Damn! Rats! But what I told you is all true; doesn't that take the place of testifying in court?" she said tearfully.

"I believe you. I really do. But you still might be called on to testify in court."

"Rats! I was not planning that at all."

"Well, you might. They might demand that you appear as a witness. That's all the questions I have for you. Do you know where the other girls are? Let's see, Moira, Samantha and Gabriella?"

"I think they're all in the coffee shop."

"Thanks for your time. And don't worry."

Cappy and Muldoon left the room at Halley Hall and headed for the coffee shop which was in the next building. When they got there, Cappy looked around and saw the girls he was looking for. They were sitting together at one of the tables. They both went over to the table. He introduced himself as a detective with the Boston police and Muldoon as his assistant.

"Hi girls. My name is Cappy. I'm a detective with the police department. This is Mr. Muldoon, my assistant. May we sit down?"

"Sure, sure take these chairs." They pointed to chairs that nobody was using. They were all apprehensive about talking to members of the Boston police.

"We wouldn't take up too much of your time. But I do have a few questions for you girls if you don't mind answering them," Cappy said as he shifted his weight in the chair.

"Sure we'll help in any way we can. I presume it's about the murder," Gabriella said. She obviously was the leader of this group of girls.

"Thanks. May I ask you where you girls were the night of the shooting?" Muldoon was busy taking notes. He thought that taking notes was beneath him as a police officer but he did it nonetheless.

"We were at the Lamppost with Megan. She stayed behind because she had asked Robert to go to the dance with her. The three of us left and went back to Megan's room in the dorm," Gabriella said.

"How come you left Megan alone?"

"We didn't want it to appear that we were in some conspiracy or plan to get him to go," Samantha said quietly.

"Did you go immediately back to the dorm, or did you stop somewhere first?"

"No, we went immediately back to the dorm," Gabriella answered.

"Were you girls in the gym the night of the dance?"

"Yes we were." Gabriella did most of the talking.

"Did you girls see or hear anything unusual at the dance?"

"No, just the gunshot and the dance music. The kids were all jumping up and down."

"So you did hear the gunshot?"

"Yeah."

"Hmmm, that's interesting. So you did hear the gunshot?"

"Yeah, we did," Gabriella answered.

"Nobody else did. Where were you guys anyhow?"

"We were all standing near the punch bowl."

"Near the punch bowl? Interesting. How come nobody else heard anything?"

"We don't know. We were just standing around when we heard the gunshot and saw everyone run to the men's room." Gabriella seemed nervous when she said this.

"You're sure about this? Hearing a shot being fired."

"Yeah, we are," Gabriella said. She said this with a bit of confidence that made Cappy feel nervous himself. Muldoon kept taking notes.

"Thanks, do you guys have any questions for me?" Cappy was visibly upset with the response that Gabriella made to his question about hearing a gunshot.

"No, nothing."

"Nothing else?" With that, Cappy and Muldoon got up from their chairs and left the building.

The girls were relieved to see them go.

CHAPTER FOURTEEN

Cappy left with Muldoon and headed back to his office. He felt that he had talked to all the students he had to see. He was tired; Muldoon was not. Cappy was focused on the difference between men and women consuming alcohol and their ability to hear. He thought that men responded to drinking in a different way than women did. Maybe, he continued to think, that is the reason that the male students at Savan were all drinking from the punch bowl the night of the murder while the girls didn't want to drink at all. They wanted only to dance. Perhaps that's why they heard a gunshot and the guys did not. There is a difference between men and women, but he did not think before this that it extended to drinking and hearing. Muldoon stood by saying nothing.

Back in his office, Cappy sat down at his desk. Muldoon remained standing beside Cappy's desk. Cappy looked at the pile of papers that were still to be read and signed. He cursed to himself that he had to read them, all of them. But he finished reading all of them and signed his name on the bottom line of each one before he printed his name beside his signature. Muldoon still remained silent.

There was only one more interview that he had to conduct. It was with Mark Iota. So far he had conducted enough interviews he thought. And he still didn't feel well. Maybe the feeling that he had was the result of something he ate. Pat was such a good cook that he couldn't imagine that it was anything that she cooked. It must have been something else. Perhaps it was the pizza he had at Pierce's house.

He finished his work and said to Muldoon that they had to go back to Savan. They got into the police car and drove to Savan again. They began to look for Iota. Cappy said that Iota had been living with Bill Galvin and Barry Sparks. It was not the policy of Savan to have three students in the same dormitory room he told Muldoon, but this year was different. There were so many students who had applied for admission to Savan that the College found it necessary that they had room for all of them. So they decided to have some rooms where three students were assigned. They called them "trips."

After searching for a while, Cappy and Muldoon found the dormitory that Iota lived in with two others whom he had already spoken to, Barry Sparks who had given mouth-to-mouth to Shaw and was already interviewed. Cappy had already spoken to Bill Galvin. They found the room and Cappy knocked on the door.

"Whose there?"

"Cappy Longquist and my assistant Sean Muldoon. We're with the Boston police. I would like to talk to Mark Iota."

"Oh sure, ok, just a minute," came the response from inside the room.

The door opened and Cappy and Muldoon went into the room. Iota was there all by himself, Galvin and Sparks, his roommates, were not there. When Cappy came in Iota just stood there. He was nervous talking to a police detective. He offered Cappy and Muldoon a seat and they sat down in two of the chairs that Iota had in the room.

"Have a seat," Iota said.

"Thanks."

"What can I do for you," you could tell that Iota was nervous. Muldoon took out his pen and notebook and was prepared to record what was said.

"I just wanted to talk to you about the murder. I have already spoken to some of the people involved. I guess I saw you there. You were standing beside the body."

"That's right. I was."

"Could you tell me why you were there?"

"Sure. I tried to catch up with him. I needed to go to the rest room too. I wished I hadn't."

"Then what happened when you got there?'

"There was a shot that came from the window. Shaw was washing his hands and I was going to the bathroom. All of a sudden a shot was fired! I heard it. It got Shaw in the back. He just crumbled over on the floor. He staggered a couple of feet and fell on his stomach. He did, he did. He just crumbled over."

"Wow!" Muldoon exclaimed. One could not tell whether he was serious when he said that.

"He just crumbled over. I wish that I didn't have to go that time."

"The window was opened?"

"Yeah, it was. I went over and looked around. I thought I saw Lane outside. I wish none of this ever happened. Why did I have to go? Right at that time?"

"Why didn't you say that you saw Lane? Or that the window was opened? Why didn't you tell me the day the murder happened? My God, why? You should have said something! It's a little important you know!"

"I don't know. I don't know. I was scared. I was scared of everything, you, Lane, the murder, all those people . . . everything!"

"You should have said something! Well, it's water under the damn now. But you should have said that you saw Lane."

"There was nothing I could have done!"

"I guess not. But you should have said that you saw Lane." Muldoon kept taking the conversation down in his notebook. He was tired.

"It was scary! And, I'm afraid of him too!"

"I'm sure that you were scared. But let me capsulize. Let me put it all together. You had to go to the men's room and caught up with Shaw, you both went in together, when Shaw finished and began was washing his hands and you heard a gunshot from outside, you looked over at Shaw and saw that he was hit in the back, he staggered and fell on the floor, you saw Lane outside, you then went over to the body and stood over it?" Cappy had a habit of summarizing his findings. He did the summarizing with all the interviews he conducted.

"That's right. About the same time Sparks came in and saw what was happening. He looked at Shaw and gave him mouth-to-mouth. He was sent to the rest room by Long."

"He was sent by Long?"

"That's right. He sent him. Sparks didn't like being told what to do but he gave Shaw mouth-to mouth. We learned how in our health class. I just stood there. I wish I hadn't had to go. I know that I said this, but I really do wish that the whole thing hadn't happened."

"That's ok. You were just standing beside the body? And you saw Lane outside? You saw him. You saw Lane, you're certain it was him. You're sure."

"That's right."

"You should have told me."

Cappy shrugged his shoulders and didn't ask Iota any more questions. Muldoon and he got up from their chairs, thanked Iota and left the room. They got the police car and headed back to the office. Cappy thought about Lane. He thought that if he was outside, he had the opportunity and the gun was available to him or belonged to him. He must be the one that fired the shot. All that was needed to make a good case against him was motive! If he found a motive, Lane must be the murderer! He was pleased with himself and now he had a suspect. It had to be Lane.

He still had a lot of paper work to do when they got to his office and the pile on his desk was growing while he was busy with his interviews. He would have to read over and over the reports that dealt with the murder at Savan and sign them. The rest of the time he could just sit there thinking. He continued to think about Lane. He got back inside the police car and returned to Savan.

While he drove, he began to trace the talks that he had with everybody that was involved. First there was Lane, the Dean of Discipline. Maybe he should have spoken to him more. He thought about that for a long time as his car almost hit a cab that was in front of him. Then there were the others, Pierce, Megan Sullivan and all of her girlfriends. And there was Galvin, Sparks, Long and finally Iota. He wondered if he had left anyone out. But he was still amazed that Iota had seen Lane outside when he went to the window and didn't mention it. What was Iota thinking, keeping this to himself? If he saw Lane outside, it contradicted what Lane had said. He said that he went right to the gym from his office.

He looked at Muldoon and saw that he was weary and told him to go home. Muldoon was glad that he did and left the car without saying another word. He got into his own car which he had parked previously in one of the parking lots that Savan kept neat and clean and went home. He lived with his dad in one of the condos that was not far away from the college. At the same time, Cappy continued to think about Lane. He knew that he had to arrest him and that Lane would have to go to trial.

"He must have been involved more so than he told me. He said that he went directly from his office to the gym," Cappy said to himself.

He looked out the window and noticed the trees outside. The leaves began to fall from the trees and they offered the walker the opportunity to crunch them while walking or to stand silently and see the wondrous colors that nature had lent. Some were red; some were green and some were yellow as they fell. He was impressed with the leaves that were falling but he kept thinking about Lane. Why didn't Iota tell him that he was outside? Was it because he was afraid of what Cappy would think that Lane was the murderer? Why did Lane tell him that he had come directly from his office? What was he hiding?

When they got back to his office, after battling the Boston traffic, Cappy went immediately to his desk. The papers that sat there were growing in number, he looked at them. He looked in horror as he read one of the papers which was a complaint that was signed by Robert Lane. Apparently, Lane had made a complaint about his wife, Lisa! His own wife! She was, according to the complaint signed by Lane, fooling around with a student at Savan and they had an intimate relationship. Cappy was shocked when he read the complaint. Could the student possibly be Shaw? Could this possibly be the motive for murder?

He commanded the two men who were assigned to him and who were just standing around to get a warrant from a judge and go to Savan and arrest Lane for murder. They leapt at this command, left the office and went to the office of Judge Arthur Kenison. They got the warrant after explaining the situation to Kenison. They got into their cars and drove to Savan. When they got there, they went immediately to Lane's office.

"Could I help you gentlemen?" The secretary was busy with her files and looked sardonically at the police officers.

"Yeah, we came to arrest Dean Lane. Don't try to interfere!"

They immediately went into his office. He was with a student. The policemen went over to where Lane was sitting and put handcuffs on him. They read him the Miranda Rights and took him out of the office. They apologized to the student but said that they were on official business and that the student should leave and go back to his classroom or to his dormitory. The student hurriedly obliged and left the office. Lane, despite his objections, was placed in the police car and taken back to the building that housed the jail. He was put into a holding cell still wondering what he was doing there. He was booked and arraigned on the charge of murder. Cappy had insisted that both procedures should be followed to the letter of the law. He insisted and they were.

"Oh my God! Could it have anything to do with the complaint I signed about my wife. Was she was having an affair with Robert Shaw! I know it was him! He was the kid who was sent to my office by Pierce! He was the boy who was shot in the men's room! Oh my God! They don't think that I had something to do with his murder! Oh my God! They can't think that!"

The guard where Lane was being held looked at him quizzically. He told Lane to be quiet that being noisy was not the best idea in the world. If he had a complaint he should take it to someone who could do something about it. At that moment, Lane made his decision; he would hire Robert B. Tell to represent him. He had heard about Tell from the Academic Dean. Tell had gone to Savan before he went to law school. He had done some legal work for Savan and the Academic Dean was very high in his praise of him.

Robert B. Tell was in his office doing paper work. He was trying to cut down the list of names of the clients he had been serving. The phone rang and he picked up the receiver.

"Hello," he said.

"Hi, I'm calling from the Oakbrook Jail! I only have three minutes to talk! That's all that they would allow me! My name is Lane; I'm the Dean of Discipline at Savan. There was a murder the other night and I think they have arrested me because of it. I would like to retain you to represent me."

"Hmm. That's interesting. But I've been trying to minimize the clients I already have." Tell was intrigued however. He had followed the murder at Savan with a great deal of interest and he thought that he would like to be involved in defending the one who was charged with this crime, whoever that was.

"I'll listen. You have three minutes. Convince me! Convince me and I'll take your case." Tell's office was very large. It had wall-to-wall carpeting, two very expensive chairs that his clients could use, a large sofa, a desk with a phone on it, and a large leather swivel chair behind the desk and costly drapes on the window. Tell was not one to quibble over the price of things.

"They have me locked up. I think that they think I had something to do with the murder."

"Did you?" Tell said briskly.

"No, I didn't! I swear on my mother's grave! I had nothing to do with the murder! I went outside trying to figure out what I should do about my wife Lisa. She was not faithful to me. She had slept with a student and I think it was Shaw. I brooded about it. The night of the murder was a good night to be walking around campus and thinking. Then I heard a shot. It seemed to come from the men's room in the gymnasium. I ran over to where I heard the shot; but I had nothing to do with the murder! You've got to believe me!"

"Ok, let me think about it." Tell hung up the phone. He often hung the phone up in the middle of a conversation. It was not unusual. He was continued to be intrigued. He recognized that he was trying to minimize his involvement with his clients, he had too many. But he was fascinated with the murder at Savan and had been following it very closely on television. After thinking about Lane's request for a long time, he came to a conclusion. He would take the case.

Lane, after hanging up the phone, was escorted back to the holding cell by the guard. The guard told him that he was doing this for the past thirty years. He complained that the officials at the jail didn't recognize his contributions, taking prisoners back and forth from the phone and then spending the day guarding them in their cell. He shook his head when he talked. Lane said nothing.

The next day Lane, after spending a sleepless night in his cell, was escorted to the court-room by the guard. Judge John O'Hara was on the bench when Lane was escorted in. Lane was dressed in an orange jump suit that all the prisoners wore and he had chains on both of his ankles. The chains forbade him to do any walking that was not approved of.

The clerk of courts ordered both Lane and his counsel, Robert B. Tell, who had accepted the invitation to represent Lane, to stand. They both did as the charge of murder in the first degree was read by the clerk of courts. Judge O'Hara took his place at the front of the courtroom. He was very stern when he looked at Lane. He said that the murder was horrific and that the guilty party or parties would have to pay a heavy price for what was done.

"What do you plead? Guilty or not guilty?" he asked.

"Not guilty!" Tell responded. Lane looked quizzically at him. He thought that Tell was over selling when he made that response. He had shouted the not guilty plea at the top of his lungs. Perhaps he should be a little more diplomatic. But Tell knew what he was doing, Lane thought.

"My client is the Dean of Discipline at Savan College and has never had even a traffic ticket. He obviously is not a threat to the community and we feel that he should not be remanded."

Tell was firm when he said this. Lane continued to stare at him. He was fascinated at the whole courtroom proceeding although, as a participant in it, he was still scared. He looked forward to being released from the courtroom. Bail was set at $250,000 and it was met by Lisa Lane. Lane thought that it might well be her who had posted the bail money.

If it was, he had a lot to say to her.

CHAPTER FIFTEEN

While Tell was thinking about his defense plan for Lane, Cappy was thinking about Lane and the murder at Savan. How could the Dean of Discipline at Savan College murder a student? It didn't make any sense. Could the student who was having the affair with Mrs. Lane possibly be Robert Shaw? If so, did that mean that Lane had a right to shoot him? It was still murder in the eyes of the law and in his mind too. There may be a difference between a sin and a crime, but murder is always wrong no matter how one looks at it.

Lane was still in jail Cappy thought as he walked toward the courthouse building where the trial was scheduled. He kept thinking that this was a bit ironic. Lane shouldn't be there. It didn't make any sense that the Dean of Discipline was going to be charged with the murder of a student. That's not what the Dean of Discipline does. He may expel a student when he feels that the student has done something that violated the college's expectations. But murder!? Never!?

He had better get a lawyer and get one quickly, Cappy thought. But Lane had already left the building that housed the jail. He was met by his wife, Lisa. They greeted one another with hugs and kisses just like any married couple; but something was amiss.

"I paid the cash that was necessary to get you out. I remortgaged the house." Lisa said sheepishly.

"I'm glad to be out of that hell hole. Thanks. But I have to ask you something. Were you having an affair with one of the students at Savan?"

"Well, ah, yes, yes I was. I'm ashamed to admit it. I'm so sorry." Lisa responded. You could tell by her shaking hands that she was very nervous.

"Is that the reason you put up the money to get me released? I should strangle you."

"I know. And I would deserve it if you did. I don't know. It just happened."

"Was the student, Robert Shaw? The kid who was murdered the other night?"

"Ah, ah, yeah it was. But I had nothing to do with the murder I didn't do anything!"

"Other than fucking him!" Lane was angry now. He was getting angrier.

"Please, please. I don't know what to say. I love you not him. I really do. It was a mistake. It was a mistake that I made! Please! It happened only once. We were at a school party, you and me. It was during freshman week and I had too much to drink. Robert came up to me. He was flirting. I know he was. He invited me upstairs. I went. I know I shouldn't have gone. I know it now, but I did. We had, ah, ah, sex. I am totally ashamed. I am so ashamed. Please forgive me. Please!" Lisa had tears in her eyes.

"I don't know. I wish I could. I did sign a complaint against you and your lover, the student. Right now, I'm glad to be here, out of that place! I don't even know why I was there! Do they think I had something to do with Shaw's death? That I was the murderer? I don't know! I don't know," he sobbed.

"Go ahead, honey, crying will make you feel better."

"Sure it will. I still should strangle you for what you did. Didn't our marriage mean anything to you? Anything at all?"

"It did and it does. Let's go home."

They left the courtyard where the courtroom building was. The trial was to take place in it. It was located near their apartment. They proceeded to go to their apartment on Commonwealth Avenue near the College. When they got there they immediately put on the television. They wanted to see the news. Did it have anything about it or the arrest of Lane? It was six o'clock and the news was just beginning. After a number of commercials, the commentator made his usual announcements then he talked about the murder at Savan and that the Dean of Discipline who had been arrested for the murder.

"The Dean of Discipline at Savan College, Mr. Robert Lane, has been charged with murder today. Mr. Lane took out a complaint against his wife Lisa prior to the murder of Robert Shaw the student who was slain. What kind of punishment system do they have at Savan anyhow? Be careful of your misbehavior students. You might be shot!"

"Turn it off," Lisa said.

"Yeah, enough is enough."

"Are you ok? The announcer said some bad things about you."

"No. He said bad things about you. How could you have been involved with a student? How could you? Don't you realize the position you've put me in? What kind of a person are you anyhow?"

"I'm sorry. I said I was sorry."

"Let's forget about it," Drew was very angry. Anyone who knew him could tell that Drew Lane was angry. He was fuming.

Drew got up from the sofa and went into the kitchen to make himself something to eat. He looked into the refrigerator but found very little. He finally decided to make a tuna sandwich. He kept thinking about Lisa and the fact that he was charged with the murder of her lover, Robert Shaw. What bothered him, almost as much as Lisa's infidelity, was that Shaw was a student! He was murdered in the men's room during a student dance in the gym!

"What is going on? What's happening to me? Why did they arrest me? It must have had something to do with Lisa and her stupid affair. It probably was related to the complaint I took out against her. I was only doing what I considered the right thing. I was taking a walk outside when I heard a shot. That's when I ran over to where the shot came from. I should have told the cops that instead of saying that I went directly to the gym. I guess I should have," he moaned.

Meanwhile, Tell was going over what he would use as a defense; he was designing his strategy. He decided that he would use the same techniques of law that worked for him in the past. He was a very good lawyer. He had gotten the names of the people that Cappy had interviewed from the prosecution, Pierce, Iota, Sparks, Galvin, and Long. Cappy had also spoken to Megan Sullivan and her girlfriends including Moira, Samantha and Gabriella. Tell would have to repeat these interviews. But he was not worried about the timing. He could do the interviews when the trial began.

The trial began with the jury chosen and Judge Romps on the bench. Romps was known for his fairness to both the defense and the prosecution. He had known Tell from their days at Savan together and he also knew him to be a fine lawyer both as a defense lawyer and as a prosecutor when Romps was first employed as an assistant to the Attorney General in the state of Massachusetts. Romps, himself, was a fine judge. He called for the opening remarks of both the prosecutor and the defense to the jury.

Tell began because both he and Dupre, the prosecutor of this case, had agreed to reverse the ordinary order of things where the prosecutor makes his statement before the defense.

"Ladies and gentlemen of the jury, my name is Robert B. Tell and I represent the defense. I will be defending Drew Lane, who is not guilty of the crime that he has been charged with. He is innocent, and I will prove it. On the night in question, knowing that there was a dance at the gymnasium at Savan, where Drew works as the Dean of Discipline, he took a walk on campus. He was concerned because he had found out that his wife was having an affair with a student. He didn't know who the student was. He didn't know his identity. It was Shaw, the victim of the murder, but he didn't know that. How then could he know at that precise time that the student whom his wife was having an affair with was in the men's room at Savan? How could he know!? Further, as the Dean of Discipline at the College, isn't it customary for the student to be expelled and not murdered when he breaks a rule of the College? He is not guilty,"

Tell had intentionally tried humor by telling the jury that the Dean of Discipline would never respond to a student's mischief by murdering him when he violates a rule of the College. It was now the prosecutor's turn to try to impress the jury. Dupre began by saying that of course the Dean of Discipline would not resort to murder when a student violates one of the rules of the College. The Dean would never do this. But under the circumstances when his wife is having an affair with the student, any man's temper would be violated and that person could resort to some form of violence even murder! And that is precisely what Drew Lane did. He is guilty, he exclaimed.

The first person called to the stand was Arthur Pierce. After he was sworn in and took the chair in the witness box, Tell asked him a few questions after the formalities of introducing himself and asking Pierce about the state of his health.

"Did you attend the dance at the gym on the night in question," Tell asked.

"No, I didn't," Pierce answered.

"Where were you?"

"I was at home watching the news on television."

"So, you were at home?"

The prosecutor, Michael Dupre, objected to the judge that the question was asked and answered. His objection was not a strong one.

"Objection sustained," the judge looked almost unconcerned.

"Fine. Then you couldn't be involved in the murder that occurred that night?" Tell was not bothered by the objection or by the judge's ruling.

"No, I was not involved in any way."

"But you didn't like Shaw, the victim, and didn't you blame him for pulling a prank on you?"

"You're right. I didn't like him at all. He was disruptive in my class and I am sure that he was involved in flooding my office."

"So you didn't like him?"

Dupre again objected saying that once again the question was asked and answered. He was getting a bit perturbed. When the judge, looking more concerned than he had been, agreed and said that the objection was sustained, Dupre took his seat.

"What's going on?" Lane whispered to Tell.

"Nothing, don't be concerned. Don't worry about anything. It was just Dupre's way of introducing himself to the court. I know you're innocent. That's all that should matter."

"Thanks. I'll be quiet from now on."

The next witness was Long who explained to the court and to both Tell and Dupre that he was Shaw's roommate and that on the night in question he had been by the punch bowl and that he had directed Sparks to go to the men's room to get Shaw and Iota; they both were taking too long. Dupre asked him if he had told others to go to the men's room and Long answered that he had not. Tell had no questions for Long.

The other witnesses were called to the witness box except for Megan Sullivan and her girlfriends and they essentially told the same story; Shaw had gone to the men's room, Iota had followed him, a shot rang out, people raced to the scene including Sparks. Sparks gave the victim mouth-to-mouth. Long called security and then the police. Tell then called Sullivan to the stand.

"Your name is Megan Sullivan, is that correct?"

"Yes it is."

"How are you today? May I ask you a few questions?"

"I'm well. Sure, you may ask me questions," she responded nervously.

"On the night in question, where were you?"

"I was, er, um, in my dormitory, Room 201 in Halley Hall."

"Were you drinking that night? Did you not take a boy to your dormitory?"

Dupre objected to this line of questioning asking where Tell was going with his questions and the relevance to the crime. The judge quickly told the court that the objection was sustained. But Tell cleverly pursued this line of questioning.

"Ok, but you did take Romano to your room. You then asked him to leave. Afterwards you found an earring missing from your jewelry box. Is that correct?"

"Yes it is."

"Could you tell us who took the single earring? Was it Romano or Shaw that took it?"

"I'm not sure who it was."

"You are not sure who took it whether it was Romano or the victim. But you were drinking the night in question?"

"Yes I was. I had too many beers at the Lamppost. I'm not accustomed to drinking."

"Is it not true that you had asked the victim to go to the dance with you on the night in question?"

"Yes it is."

"Thank you. No further questions of the witness at this time."

Tell was suggesting that maybe the witness was responsible for Shaw's death. At least, he hoped that the jury would see it that way. Dupre was getting irritated at this line of questioning and asked Tell where he was going with all these inquiries. Tell said that the earring was an important part of his case and that he intended to pursue it. He also said that maybe Ms. Sullivan had something to do with the murder. He had gotten what he wanted.

"Your witness," Tell was almost gleeful when he said this.

"Hi Miss Sullivan." Dupre said with an air of authority. "Tell me, did you have anything to do with the murder? Anything at all?" He wanted to meet Tell's influence on the jury.

"No I did not." Megan was firm in her response.

"You said that you had too many beers at the Lamppost. You are not accustomed to drinking are you?"

"No I'm not."

"And you said that there was an earring missing from your jewelry box. Is it possible that you left it at home?"

"Yes, it's possible. I really don't remember. I must not have since Detective Cappy found it."

"Thank you. Nothing further." With that, Dupre went back to his seat.

Tell then called Cappy to the stand. His attempt to link Megan Sullivan to the crime had been upended by the question that Dupre had asked of her, or so Tell thought. But Tell was not finished yet. He had thought of all the possibilities before going to the jury trial.

"Your name is Detective Clyde Longquist?"

"That's right."

"Do you have anything to tell the court?" Tell was being very evasive.

"I do. I interviewed all the witnesses to the crime; at least I thought I got them all. And I went to Miss Sullivan's dorm room at Halley Hall and looked around. I went to her jewelry box and looked inside. I saw that she was missing an earring. It was a match to the one I found in Shaw's pocket when I went through his trousers. I took the one that I found on Shaw to the lab. I wanted to find out if it had anything to do with the murder."

"And what did the lab tell you?"

"The lab said that it was Miss Sullivan's. They found DNA on it that matched hers."

"I see. I hold the option of calling this witness back," he said to the judge.

"Very well," the judge said. "The witness is excused."

Tell then called the students who were interviewed by Cappy. Galvin, Iota, Sparks, Long and the girls who were friendly with Sullivan were all interviewed. He asked them if they had heard a shot from the men's room and whether or not they were involved in the murder. The students all said that they were not, in any way, involved in the murder and the female students all said that they heard a shot while the male students had said that they heard nothing. Tell attributed the difference to the fact that the men had been drinking and the woman had not. Alcohol tends to reduce ones relationship with the environment. Tell believed this with all his heart and his soul; his older brother, after all, was an alcoholic. Tell might have been right. He might have been wrong.

When Tell was finished asking questions of the students, Dupre responded to the judge's invitation and asked the students where they were and whether or not they had anything to do with the murder of Shaw. The students all said that they had nothing to do with this horrible crime and that they would be happy when the trial was over; nonetheless, they all said that it would impact on the rest of their lives. Dupre said that he agreed. The students were all excused from the witness stand. Some took their seats in the courtroom while the others left. Then Tell called Lane to the witness stand. He took the oath to tell all that he knew about the crime and swore to tell the truth.

"Your name is Drew Lane and you are the Dean of Discipline at Savan, is that correct." Tell was beginning to feel a bit exhausted.

"That's correct."

"Could you tell me where you were on the night in question?"

"I was in my office and decided to take a walk outside. I stopped for a moment by the men's room at the gym. Only for a moment though, and then I proceeded to go on my walk."

"Is it usual for you to go out of your office for a walk?"

"No it isn't."

"Why then was the night in question an exception?"

"I wanted to clear my mind."

"Why is that?"

"Umm, err. My wife was having an affair with a student. I signed a complaint with the police. It might have been Shaw. It might have been someone else. But I had nothing to do with his murder! Please believe me. Nothing at all. I was just walking to clear my mind. I did hear, I think, some noise from the men's room but I thought nothing of it."

"So you only went for a walk to clear your mind?"

Dupre immediately objected to the question that Tell had asked saying that the question was asked and answered. The judge agreed with him and sustained the objection. Dupre was becoming increasingly irritated with Tell and the technique of asking a question and then repeating it. Tell on the other hand, was almost gleeful that Dupre had reacted just as he planned. The trial went as Tell had wanted. In closing, Tell suggested that Lane had gone for a walk to clear his head about Lisa and the student, whoever it was, and had nothing to do with Shaw's murder. How could he? He asked the jury to think a little bit how Lane would know that Shaw would be in the men's room at that precise time and how would he know that Shaw was the one whom Lisa was having the affair with, if he was the one. It didn't make any sense he told the jury.

Dupre, on the other hand, tried to convince the jury that Lane was the murderer. He said that Lisa was indeed having an affair with Shaw and that Lane knew it. He knew it. He had the gun that he had taken from home, and it just happened that he saw Shaw in the men's room through the window when Shaw had to use the bathroom. He fired the gun once, the bullet hit Shaw and he died from the wound. Lane then threw the gun to the ground and then he raced as fast as he could to the dance inside.

"I trust that you will find him guilty of his horrific crime," he ended his presentation to the jury.

The jury didn't take long. They deliberated for only two hours, both attorneys and Long's family waited in the room next to the courtroom. The room was ordinarily flooded with lawyers, now there were only two and, of course, Long's family. They were all summoned into the courtroom in a short period of time. The jury's foreman, an elderly gentleman, gave the verdict, written on a slip of paper to the clerk of courts. The slip of paper had Lane's future written on it. It was handed to the judge who looked nonchalantly at it and he then gave it back to the clerk of courts to read. The slip of paper read not guilty of the crime of murder. The jury had found Lane not guilty of the crime. The defendant Lane hugged Tell and then the other members of his family including Lisa. Tell was pleased with himself while Dupre was very upset. Dupre however shook hands with Tell, and then he stormed out of the room. Tell told Lisa that she had better be careful with her behavior and he shared his glee with the other members of the Lane family. Lane was ecstatic at the verdict but he looked at his wife sternly.

"You realize, I hope, that none of this would have happened if you did not have an affair with a student."

Lisa looked ashamed at Lane saying this and said that, although it was Shaw, she was very happy that the jury had come up with the verdict that had exonerated her husband. They both hugged one another and kissed. Lane had seemingly forgiven her for her indiscretion. From outward appearances it would seem to be the case. They had kissed when the verdict was read and they left the courthouse together, hand in hand. Tell was still relishing his victory as he picked up his papers from the table that he was sitting at and he left the building.

The courtroom was now quiet.

Chapter Sixteen

Lisa and Drew went back to their apartment. Drew was relieved that the jury had found him innocent but he was still distressed at Lisa. He yelled at her that he would not be in the predicament that he was in if it were not for her and her dalliance with a student. A student, he shouted. Didn't she understand? How could she be unfaithful to him? Why didn't she understand his predicament? Drew made these and other statements to her. Lisa was apologetic. She said that she was so very sorry. Drew yelled at her, the more apologetic she became.

Meanwhile, Cappy had gone home to his wife and twins in Charlestown. He felt that he needed to get away from police work for a while. His wife, Pat, and the twins greeted him when he got there. Pat had made her famous spaghetti for dinner. After he ate, he did his usual things and went to bed. The next day, feeling rested from a good night's sleep, he went to his office in the Back Bay. When he got there, his men were all talking about the trial and that Lane had been exonerated of the crime. They were pleased that he was. Cappy, accustomed to trials of this kind, remained silent. He had no interest in talking to his men about it. No interest whatsoever. His interest was only in finding the killer of Shaw. Whatever the result of any future trial relating to Shaw and his murder, he was intent on bringing his killer to justice.

Cappy began his day thinking about the crime. He was still interested in the earring that he had found in Shaw's pocket when he searched him. He wondered where he had gotten it. Did Megan Sullivan give it to him? Had he taken it? He could not get the earring out of his mind. He was obsessed with it. He picked up his phone and called the crime lab. The crime lab assistant answered and Cappy asked him to check the DNA profile that was sent to him. The assistant confirmed that it was Sullivan's earring when he checked; it could not belong to anyone else. Cappy thanked him and was determined to find out why he had found it in Shaw's pocket. He couldn't think of anything else. He was obsessed. He thought he should speak to Sullivan again.

Lane and Pierce had returned to their jobs at Savan. Lane thought that he should be more affectionate to Lisa when the opportunity presented itself. And Pierce thought that he should be more responsive to student's needs. All the students who were interviewed by Cappy went back to their studies or to their dorms. Things appeared to be normal again at Savan College. Nobody talked about Shaw and the night that he was murdered, nor did anybody speak about Sparks, Long, Galvin, Iota or Sullivan and any of her girlfriends. Everything was like it was before the incident in the gym. The students were studying underneath the many trees that were at Savan and were still changing colors. Many of the professors were teaching their classes there.

Cappy, however, was still thinking about the earring that he had found in Shaw's pocket the night he was killed and Lane, although he was not worried any more about a trial and vowed that he would be more affectionate to his wife, was busy in his office talking to students who had been sent there. The Board of Directors had returned him to his office despite the general feeling that he should not return to the post that he had. He said at the trial that he had gone for a walk on that night to clear his mind. He had heard commotion coming from the men's room in the gym, he had run to the area and saw a gun on the ground, but he said that he had nothing to do with the crime. He didn't even have a gun, he claimed.

Although everything had the appearance of being normal, things were not what they appeared. Many students, prompted by their parents, had decided to leave Savan and transfer to another school

Tell was back at his office going over the trial and thinking about his victory over Dupre. He was pleased with himself. But he could not figure out the relevance of Sullivan's earring either. Both he and Cappy were on the same wave line when it came to the earring. Both had wondered whether Sullivan had given the earring to Shaw or whether he had taken it. If she had given the earring to him what did it mean? If he had taken it, then why did he? Tell was wondering about these issues just as Cappy was. All of a sudden the phone rang in Tell's office.

"Hello," Tell said.

"You don't know who I am but I have something to tell you."

"Go ahead. I'm listening."

"Did you know that Shaw had taken the earring from Sullivan's jewelry box so that he could impress the guys who were at the dance?"

"Oh? No I didn't know that."

"He did." With that the person who had made the call hung up the phone.

Cappy had made the call only because he wanted Tell to be aware that Shaw took the earring from Sullivan's jewelry box. He kept thinking about the earring. He thought about it consistently. Probably he took it to show the other guys and to prove that he had a date with her. Tell attempted to get a trace on the call by having his secretary monitor it. The caller was male, that's all that she knew. She was not successful in tracing the call and had no experience in doing this kind of work. And the caller had hung up very quickly anyhow. Tell looked at her and said that he frequently got prank calls and that he was just thinking about the earring when the phone rang. He said that it must have been a coincidence that he was thinking about it at the very moment that the phone rang.

Meanwhile, Sparks, Galvin, Long and Iota were talking about the murder while they drank coffee in the coffee shop. They all thought that it was a horrible tragedy. Long appeared to be especially distressed. He was Shaw's roommate. Sparks, who had given Shaw mouth to mouth resuscitation, made the comment that Shaw may have been too much in a hurry when he went to the men's room that dreadful night. He said that if Shaw had not gone to the men's room when he did, he probably would still be alive today. Galvin looked the glummest of all of them and asked if they could please talk about something else.

Although his friends considered him odd and mouthy, Iota just sat there without saying a word. It was very much like he stood in the men's room over Shaw's body the night that he was killed. He was speechless. But he was thinking about that night.

Bob Shaw had drunk from the punch bowl and then said that he had to go to the men's room. Iota followed after him. When they got to the men's room, Iota began the conversation.

"So, you brought a girl to the dance."

"I did! I did! I surely did! And I have her earring to prove it. I do, I have her earring. I have her earring. Look, look at it! Look! I also slept with a woman! I did! She loved it! She did! She might be the wife of someone you know! Ha!"

Shaw was gloating at Iota when he talked and showing Iota the earring. He took it out of his pocket and began to dance around teasingly. He danced and danced putting one foot in front of the other. He danced around intentionally. He kept teasing Iota about the earring that he had stolen from Sullivan's jewelry box. He finished dancing around and he put the earring back in his pocket.

"I have a girlfriend, hah, hah!"

"You son-of-a-bitch! You were supposed to be true to me and true to me only! I put myself on the line for you. I gave up everything for you. You don't need a woman. I am the only person you need! I am your boyfriend!"

"I know. I know, I should have been true to my boyfriend," he said sarcastically. He said this as he finished with what he was doing and went to the sink to wash his hands. He whistled all the while that he washed at the sink. Iota, as angry now that he had ever been in his life, took out the gun from his pocket and fired once. The bullet hit Shaw in the back. He felt a terrible pain. He turned and looked blankly at Iota. Then he collapsed on the floor of the empty men's room. He saw only black. He was dead.

Iota had taken the gun from the display case that his father had. His dad was proud of his collection of guns. He used to praise the founders who wrote the Second Amendment to the Constitution, even though the second Amendment applied to states raising a militia. The Supreme Court had ruled that people had a right to have a gun. That is what the meaning of the Second Amendment was, they said. Mark's dad was very proud of the writers of this Amendment, almost as proud as he was of owning the guns that he had in his collection.

Mark Iota had taken the gun, plus bullets, because he wanted to impress the other guys at the dance. He thought that by having a loaded gun to show them they would stop all the comments that they made about him being gay.

They did not know that Shaw was gay and had been intimate with Iota, or that he and Shaw were boyfriends. They just thought that they were good friends, just like the rest of them.

When Iota had realized what he had done, he quickly threw the gun out the half-open window and stared blankly at the corpse of Robert Shaw. He wanted to blame someone else for what he had done. Perhaps he could say that someone was hiding in one of the stalls.

Suddenly, all hell broke loose and people were coming into the men's room, both male and female. They couldn't believe what they were looking at. Gabriella was there along with Samantha and Moira. Megan Sullivan was there too. The girls were screaming and the guys looked as though someone had just punched them in the stomachs. Just then, Long came in as Sparks began to administer the mouth-to-mouth resuscitation that they had been taught in their health class. Sparks had come into the men's room before Long. Long shouted that someone had better call the police and he ran out of the room to call campus security. Finally the police came. This was Iota's introduction to Cappy.

While Iota was sheepishly listening to the guys talking about the night of Shaw's murder, Cappy was putting the phone down. He had just made a call to Tell and told him that he should be interested in the earring. Both he and Tell knew that the earring belonged to Sullivan but Tell didn't know that Shaw had taken it from her jewelry box. Cappy thought that he should be aware of this if he were to represent someone else for the murder at Savan.

Tell, in the meantime, went back to his work. He was intrigued by the phone call that he received and wondered who he would represent the next time. Even though he was busy, he was intent on finding the next person to defend in the Savan murder.

Iota had told nobody about both the murder and the fact that he and Shaw had a homosexual relationship. He was intent on remaining silent about both of these. He felt that if he confessed to the murder, which he was tempted to do on the very night that he had committed the crime, he would be further ostracized from the other students; and if he admitted that Shaw and he had a homosexual relation the other guys would tease him and they would hate him. It was not for any moral reason that he didn't come forth with his guilt about both things but it was only in consideration of the other "guys".

Iota left the others, Long, Sparks and Galvin, and went back to his dormitory. He was still plagued with guilt about the murder, not guilty because he had done something terribly wrong when he pulled the trigger of the gun or about his homosexual relation with Shaw. His only concern was about the "guys" and what their opinion of him would be if they knew that he was the murderer.

When he got to his room, he went immediately to his closet and took out several ties. He thought that seven, tied together, would be sufficient for him. He was intent on committing suicide. He was intent on taking his own life. He thought that by making a loop of the ties that he would be successful. He got a chair from in front of his desk and stood on it. When he had completed the task of making a loop with the ties, he placed the loop around his neck. They were now like one piece of rope. He strung the ties to a steel rod that held the ceiling together. He jumped from the chair. The steel rod broke and he fell to the floor. He screamed at the ties and at himself. He shouted that he could not do anything right, not even take his own life.

When Sparks and Galvin returned from the coffee shop [Long had gone to his own room], they found Iota wrapped up very much like a ball of twine. They both tried getting him to speak but to no avail. They looked at the steel rod that had fallen and the ties that Iota had around his neck and both of them began to scream at Iota. They yelled at him and asked what the hell he was thinking of. Iota himself was still plagued with a hurricane of guilt. Iota began to cry.

Both Sparks and Galvin did all that they could to show that they were still his friends despite anything that he might have done. But he resisted them, clinging to the fact that his suicide attempt was not successful. He told them both that he was a failure in life, a failure about everything. He could not even be successful in his attempt to commit suicide. He felt like such a failure. Then he talked about his relationship with Shaw. He said that he was a failure there as well. He told them about Shaw's homosexuality and his own. At first they did not believe him about Shaw but gradually they were convinced. They were shocked more about his confession concerning Shaw than they were about his admission about his homosexuality. They both said that they knew he was gay from the very first time that they met him. But it didn't make any difference. They immediately liked him and were pleased when he had shown up to be their roommate. But they were unaware that Shaw was gay. That surprised them.

When Iota asked them how they felt knowing that he was homosexual. They both paused for a moment and repeated that they knew from the first time that they met him that he was gay, but it was not important. As long as he didn't try to influence others, they were glad to have him as a roommate. Just as long as he didn't try anything fishy or funny, they weren't terribly concerned. They said that a person's sexuality was so private and so important to a person's identity that they should not get involved. They both said that the same is true of everyone. Nobody should judge another person just because of his or her sexuality. Besides, they liked Iota.

Still they were shocked about Shaw. He had appeared to be so much in charge of everybody as well as of himself and he seemed so much attracted to the girls at Savan that nobody would suspect that he was homosexual. And they had a suspicion that he had an affair with someone, some girl or lady. Perhaps he was bi-sexual they thought, but they both said that they didn't care.

Let a person do what the person seems comfortable with and all will be fine. They asked Iota if he was going to be ok. Sparks and Galvin were both concerned that he might repeat the attempted suicide if they left him alone. He got up from the floor and told both of them that he was fine. He said that he was ok. He was feeling much better than he had felt and was grateful for their help and understanding. He was relieved to find out that they both knew about his homosexuality but that they liked him anyhow. Both Sparks and Galvin breathed a sigh of relief.

Iota said that he felt like going to the coffee shop and having a cup of coffee and a bite to eat. He said, half smilingly, that attempting to commit suicide was hard work and he needed food. Sparks and Galvin didn't know what to say about this idea, but they went along with him.

They said that they didn't like the idea, but if he was intent on going to the coffee shop, they would go with him. When they got there, all three ordered coffee and an assortment of sandwiches.

Arthur Peirce was also in the coffee shop having coffee. He was thinking about the trial and the meeting that he had with the Sullivan girl in his office. He thought that his meeting with her was strange. He thought that it was even stranger that she did not want anybody to hear about her meeting with him. He wondered why.

When he saw Iota, Sparks and Galvin were by themselves, he beckoned them to come over to his table. All three looked at one another but they complied with Pierces wishes. Students often do what a professor wishes them to do even when they don't want to.

"Hi Mr. Pierce, how yah doin' today?" They all seemed to be speaking in unison.

"Fine, I'm fine, no problems, sit down, sit down, please."

They accepted the invitation and sat down. They were immediately at a loss about what to say to Pierce. They felt uncomfortable. Students often not only do what a professor wants them to, but also they are tongue tied when they attempt to say anything to him. Pierce broke the silence by asking them what they were doing today. The weather was great and the sun was shining.

"So, what are you guys doin' today?"

"Nothing much," Sparks answered as he took the fork out of his mouth. He suspected that Pierce knew that they were involved in the break in in his office but Pierce had said nothing about it. Instead, Pierce began to converse with them about the trial and what his opinion of Lane was. He thought that Lane was victimized by his wife, Lisa, and that he should never have been charged with the murder of Shaw. Lane, to him, was a good and decent man. The three students disagreed and responded that Lane was a bad apple and he treated students with a lack of respect when he talked to them. Pierce did not agree with this way of thinking. He said that students didn't take their responsibilities seriously and Lane's job was to punish student misbehavior. The three students finished their sandwiches, excused themselves and left the table. Pierce was left to his own devices. Sparks looked back at him and smiled. The others took their trays over to the dishwasher and placed them there.

Pierce said to himself that student's thinking that they should be treated respectfully was a far cry from when he attended college. He thought that students were overly concerned about their own position and not fully understanding of the administration's. When the students left he just shrugged his shoulders and resumed eating his lunch.

"Boy, things never change," Sparks said.

"They sure don't," Iota responded as he left the table, still not fully recovered from his suicide attempt. He thought that the other students would not understand. They would not understand his homosexuality, nor would they understand his relationship with Shaw. He didn't tell Sparks and Galvin that it was he who was responsible for the murder of Shaw. That he was the one who fired the gun. That he was the murderer. But he did tell them why he attempted to take his own life. He thought that nobody else would understand, certainly not the other students nor the faculty. Suicide is always frowned upon by others. Students don't understand why any person would attempt to take his own life. They all say that they would never have the courage to do that.

Iota, Sparks and Galvin went back to their room in the dormitory. When they got there, they all looked at the ceiling that Iota's attempt at taking his life had destroyed and they wondered what to do about it. They immediately thought that maybe they could take care of the damage themselves rather than to call maintenance to do it since the responsibility was on the students to take care of any damage that was done to a room.

In the meantime, Cappy was still thinking about the murder at Savan. He thought about the earring and wondered why he had found it in one of Shaw's pockets. What was it doing there? What was the relationship between Shaw and Megan Sullivan who owned the earring? His thoughts kept running over the same things when the captain of detectives asked him what he thought about Muldoon and what he thought about Lane's trial. He said that he was pleased with Muldoon and he told the captain that he had no thoughts about the outcome one way or the other about the trial. He felt that the jury had done its job and they considered whether Lane was guilty or innocent. His only concern was to tell the truth as he understood it when he testified. He had done the right thing he thought and Lane's acquittal was not of concern to him. The captain simply shrugged his shoulders and walked away.

Cappy's thoughts were still on the earring. Did Sullivan give Shaw the earring or did he take it?

He picked up the phone and called the criminal lab again. He inquired about the report of the DNA. Unsure of himself, he inquired if the lab was positive about the identification of Sullivan owning the earring. When they assured him that they were positive about their findings, he hung up the phone still baffled about the relationship between Shaw and Sullivan. Was the earring at all related to the crime?

Tired from his thoughts about it, he decided to go home to Charlestown. When he got there, he was greeted by his wife Pat and the twins Calie and Kasie. They announced that dinner would soon be ready. Pat was cooking shrimp. When he ate and did his usual things, he went to bed. Feeling rested the next day, he drove off to his office in the Back Bay section of Boston. Even though the Boston traffic was still heavy, he didn't get upset with all the cars as he usually did. It was not like him at all, but he hummed one of his favorite tunes as he drove. He arrived at his office and immediately began thinking about the earring. Maybe it was not related to the crime at all. Maybe Sullivan had given it to him and had forgotten about it. Maybe what she said at Lane's trial about possibly leaving it at home was correct. Maybe it was not related at all.

CHAPTER SEVENTEEN

After greeting his men, Cappy picked up the phone on his desk and again called the crime lab. He again asked the person who answered if the lab was sure about identifying Sullivan. The person who answered the phone was getting annoyed at all the phone calls that Cappy had made, and he told him so. When he got assurance that the lab was absolutely positive about identifying Sullivan and the earring, he put the phone down and looked around the room to make sure that nobody saw or heard him. He was not confident at all about the earring and didn't want anybody to notice it. But he did feel better about the whole thing now that he called the lab again, despite the critical problem with his calls with the lab. He now felt that he had to speak to Sullivan. He picked up the phone again and called her.

"Hello," was the response on the other end of his call.

"This is Cappy Longquist of the Boston police. Could I ask you a few questions?"

"Sure. Oh hi," she said.

"It's about the earring that I found in one of Shaw's pocket. To tell you the truth, I am obsessed with it. Could you answer some questions about it?"

"Sure."

"Could you tell me if you left the earring home or did you give it to Shaw?"

"Neither one. As I said in the trial of Dean Lane, I couldn't remember leaving it home, but I am very sure that I didn't give it to him."

"Is it possible that he took it from your room?"

"Sure, anything is possible. I did leave the door unlocked and he may have come in and took the earring from the jewelry box. I don't know. What is the problem? Why the concern about the earring?"

"How's the investigation going anyhow?"

"Thanks. Oh, the investigation is going fine. Thanks for asking. And thanks for the info on Shaw and the earring. I'm sure that it will help," Cappy responded before hanging up the phone.

Shaw must have taken it. He must have. When he was completely satisfied that Shaw had taken the earring, even though it was his own thought process that had arrived at this conclusion, he thought that it put a different light on the investigation.

In the meantime, Megan Sullivan was brooding about her involvement in the Shaw murder. In fact, she moaned about it. Since there were no classes scheduled for Monday, she decided to go home to Connecticut. Hastily, she went to her closet and packed one of her bags. She picked up the phone which was in her room and called the ticket agency for the railroad. She was assured that there would be sufficient room for her on the 3:00pm train and she made reservations on it. She took her bag, called a cab and went to the station. She boarded the train to Connecticut and took her seat by the window. A young man came on the train a little while later and took a seat beside her.

When the train started, she looked out the window as the city of Boston with all its glamour. Its surroundings passed by her. She continued to stare as the train picked up speed and finally the young man said something.

"Excuse me, but I noticed your book cover and it says that it is a novel by Kurt Vonnegut. Are you a student?"

"Yes I am."

"Oh, do you go to Savan? I was a student there. I graduated last year."

"That's nice."

"Are you in the mood for some conversation?"

"Not really."

"Something else then?"

"Get lost!"

She obviously wanted to be left alone with her thoughts but the young man persisted. He indicated that he was employed in the software market. It didn't make any difference to her and she told him. She was nonresponsive to his flirtations. She obviously was not interested in anything that he had to say as train pulled into the Connecticut station. When it did, she left her seat and took her bag with her. She exited the train after smiling at the young man. It was a phony smile. She called a cab. She indicated the address that she wanted the cabbie to take. The address that she gave him was her home.

Her home was magnificent. It was built in the previous century. It was very ornate. After paying the cab fare and giving the cabbie a very generous tip, she climbed the stairs and went in the front door. When her mother saw her, she screamed with delight and wondered why she was home when she was supposed to be at Savan in Boston.

"My, my; my girl is home," she said as she hugged Megan.

"Hi mother," she said hugging her tightly.

"I am so happy to see you! It doesn't seem that long ago that your father and I took you up to Boston. You look wonderful. How come you are home? Don't give me any bad news. Don't. I know about the murder that took place at your school. It's such a tragedy. It was all over the news here in Connecticut. It's the only thing that they reported on. My poor darling, I hope you didn't have anything to do with it."

Megan assured her that nothing was wrong with her. She simply wanted to get home for a while and take a break from everything, especially the murder that had occurred at Savan. Her mother said that she understood and would make tea for them both and then they could talk. Despite everything, she was delighted to have her daughter home. Megan had all that she could to refrain from tears but smiled at her mother and said that she was tired and wanted to go to her room. Megan gave her mother a big hug.

Mrs. Spinoza, the next door neighbor, rang the front doorbell and Mrs. Sullivan let her in. When Megan was younger, she would go next door to the Spinoza's house and play with Mrs. Spinoza's girls. They were quite a bit older now and playing games was the last thing on their minds, or on her mind. The Spinoza girls, Harriet and Amy, were just a year apart and they now went to Providence College. When they were five or maybe six years old, they would play with their dolls and play all sorts of games with Megan. Megan had not seen them for a couple of years now and she missed the fun that they used to have. Megan played games with Mr. and Mrs. Spinoza too. Mrs. Spinoza was always good to Megan and Mr. Spinoza was truly a very good man. One of Megan's favorite games was "pins the tail on the donkey." Mr. and Mrs. Spinoza were always good to be around. It was fun then, but now more serious things were important. When a person gets older, his or her values change and what at one time would have been quite acceptable is now quite foreign to them. Megan recognized this, but at this moment in time, she would have given all that she had to play again with Harriet, Amy and Mr. and Mrs. Spinoza.

Megan went to her room after saying hello to Mrs. Spinoza and inquiring about Harriet and Amy. When she got there, she began to cry. They were silent tears that she shed. While she couldn't undo what had been done, she regretted ever going to the Lamppost and especially regretted what she had done to Robert Shaw; she should never have pretended that she wanted to go to the dance with him. She should never have gone to her dorm room with Romano and his flirtation was silly she thought. She felt that she was a bad person. She should never have done the things that she did. If only there was some way to undo the past and construct it the way that you wished things were. And what about the single earring that detective Cappy was so intent about. Had she left it at home? She went to her jewelry box on the night stand beside her bed and looked for it. She saw that the other earring was not there. She felt that because she had one earring in her jewelry box at school, the other one must be at school as well. Maybe Shaw took it. Probably he did.

There was a small bathroom off the bedroom that she had. She took all the prescription medications from the medicine cabinet and mixed them all together. She was very depressed. She, after looking at them for a long time, put them into her mouth. She ingested the entire mix of pills. Then she lay down on her bed. After she once again wished that she hadn't had anything to do with the Lamppost or Shaw or Romano and his flirtation, or the young man on the train, she closed her eyes. In the next instant she was dead.

There was a knock on the door and Mrs. Sullivan came in saying that tea was being served downstairs. Mrs. Spinoza was still there and would be joining them she said. When she saw Megan lying there unresponsive and looked at the medication bottles strewn over the bed, she began to scream. She looked at Megan and her screams got louder.

"Oh no! Oh my God! No, no, oh my God! Megan, Megan wake up! Please!"

Megan was dead. She was a victim of her own hand but also she was victimized by Shaw and Savan and the murder that occurred there. She was also victimized by the young man on the train. Mrs. Sullivan kept screaming for her to wake up. Mrs. Spinoza ran up the stairs and burst into the room shouting what was wrong, what had happened. She was told that Megan must have taken all the medication on the bed and that she must have committed suicide. Mrs. Spinoza screamed together with Mrs. Sullivan. They both screamed. Neither one could believe what they were seeing.

"My God! Oh, my God!" Mrs. Spinoza kept saying.

Mrs. Sullivan went to the phone that was on the night table beside Megan's bed and called 911. The operator told her to stay on the line and that she would send medics out to the house. When the medics got there, they tried to revive the body but to no avail. Mrs. Sullivan was near hysterics while they were doing this and Mrs. Spinoza was as pale as a zombie. When the medics said that they were sorry but there was nothing more they could do, Mrs. Sullivan fainted. The medics gave her smelling salts while Mrs. Spinoza went to the phone to call Mr. Sullivan. She told him the bad news that Megan had killed herself and that his wife had fainted. Mr. Sullivan could not accept this and said that she had to be kidding. Mrs. Spinoza finally persuaded him that she was not, and Mr. Sullivan felt that he might faint. He had loved Megan as much as a father should love his daughter. He didn't faint. But he almost did. While Mr. Sullivan tried to fathom Megan taking her own life, Mrs. Spinoza called her own husband at his office. He answered the phone and when she told him what had happened, he collapsed. The other people in his office rushed to his side and administered to him. He was very close to Megan. In fact, often Mr. Spinoza was seen as closer to her than her own father was.

Meantime, while all this was happening, Cappy was in his office looking at his desk. He had a blank expression on his face. He kept thinking about the earring and its significance to the murder. He thought that it was strange to have only one earring in Megan's jewelry box at school. Suddenly the phone rang. After he said hello and asked who was calling, the voice on the other end told him that Megan Sullivan had committed suicide. It was Gabriella LaRocha who called. She was crying. She called because she wanted to call and because Cappy had a right to know whatever details that could make his investigation go smoothly. Megan could not be a suspect in the murder. She was dead. Besides the other girls, Moira Larkin and Samantha Lavine had convinced Gabriella to call. Cappy was shocked at the news that Gabriella told him over the phone. He looked confused and dumbfounded. He couldn't believe what he was hearing. He thought that Megan could not be dead, that she could not have committed suicide; someone must have gotten it wrong. Gabriella must be mistaken. She must be.

When he hung up the phone, he asked himself why she would have committed suicide. She had so much to live for. Certainly the earring that he was obsessed with must have had something to do with it. He had convinced himself that the earring was an important part of his investigation and he was determined to find out what significance it had. Maybe she gave Shaw the earring and felt guilty about it. Maybe he took it. He didn't know the answer to this but was determined to find out what had happened. Megan's suicide had further prodded him to look at all possibilities. Why was the earring important? Or was it?

Gabriella was dating Barry Sparks at the time that she placed the call to Cappy. Sparks, of course, was rooming with Iota and Galvin when Shaw was shot. They frequently talked about the murder and the fact that Sparks had given Shaw mouth-to-mouth resuscitation in the hope of reviving him. They thought that the murder, and then Sparks giving Shaw mouth-to-mouth was weird. Galvin did most of the talking when they discussed the murder. Iota was silent when they spoke about the shooting. Sometimes Galvin and Sparks spent their entire evenings talking about the murder. One night, when Sparks was walking Gabriella back to her dormitory, they were approached by Iota who asked them a question about the murder of Shaw and the suicide of Sullivan. He asked them if Sparks had seen the gun that was outside the window of the men's room the night of the murder. And did Sparks notice the earring in Shaw's pocket. When he was told by Sparks that he was too busy trying to resuscitate Shaw and that he saw nothing else, Iota said that he felt that Sparks had told him everything he knew. Iota looked strange Sparks felt.

Sparks and Gabriella remained where they were standing when Iota had left. Sparks scratched his head and wondered why Iota would ask him the question about seeing the gun and the suicide of Sullivan. He wondered why Iota had asked him the question of whether or not he had seen the earring. He thought that it was a very strange question for Iota to ask. He generally thought that Iota was a very strange person.

Gabriella agreed with him, but she kept thinking about Megan committing suicide. Why did she do it? She had so much to live for. She was beautiful, bright and popular. Why? Why? She couldn't get free from these thoughts.

They continued their walk back to her dormitory. Just then a black cat walked in front of her. She giggled a bit and said that it was bad luck to have a cat walk in front of you, especially if it was a black one. Barry laughed at this suggestion and they continued to walk to her dormitory. Barry was still thinking about meeting Iota when Bill Galvin and Steve Long walked by them. Barry said hi, but they did not return the greeting. Later Sparks would find out that the reason that they did not return the greeting was because they did not like Gabriella.

When Barry and she got to her dormitory and he said goodnight to her, he ran to catch up with Galvin and Long. When he got there, he asked them why they had not returned his greeting. They said that they didn't like Gabriella at all. That was the only reason that they gave although Barry was still suspicious. He thought there were other reasons. Maybe, he thought, they had suspicion that he had committed the murder. After all, he was in the men's room before the crowd had come to look at the crime. Even though he was performing mouth-to-mouth, he could have shot Shaw beforehand. Or maybe they were upset about his involvement in flooding Pierce's office. When they did flood his office, Barry was not thrilled with the idea that they put water all over the place. Maybe that was it, but he could not have been the murderer. He was the one who discovered the body and gave him mouth to mouth resuscitation. How could he be the murderer when he was the one who found the body and Iota was just standing there? It didn't make any sense. But, he accepted what Galvin and Long had said that they simply did not like Gabriella.

They both said that she was too bossy.

Chapter Eighteen

When Gabriella got to her dorm, she was greeted by Moira Larkin and Samantha Lavine. They both had red eyes from the tears that they shed when they heard about Megan's suicide. When they saw Gabriella they broke into tears again and both of the girls sobbed and hugged her. They said that they were so sorry for her and felt so badly for Megan and for her. After all, they said, Gabriella was Megan's roommate and now the room was so lonely. In addition, they said that anybody who takes his or her own life just doesn't have courage enough to face reality. They were sympathetic, but they wondered why it had happened. When their greeting was ended and sympathies were shared, Moira and Samantha returned to their own dorm room leaving Gabriella alone for the first time since Megan had taken her life. Gabriella looked around her room and burst into tears. The room looked so barren. She was afraid to be there all alone. She missed Megan so much. She missed her smile, her personality, which at times was so flighty, and she missed Megan the person. She had been so accustomed to her and to having her in the room that now it seemed so unreal, so lonely. She went to the phone and called the supervisor of Halley Hall and requested another room.

The supervisor was sympathetic but said that the only rooms that he had were currently occupied by other students and that transferring her to another room would mean that Savan College would have three students in a room rather than two. But under the circumstances, he was willing to put her into another room. Gabriella said that both Moira and Samantha were both friendly with her and Megan. The supervisor said that he was willing to transfer her there, but only for the rest of the semester. He said that he had no option since Savan was so harsh on anyone who deviated from the expectation that the college have only two per room even though sometimes it was not followed. In fact, they did have "trips". He said that under the circumstances, nobody would complain. Gabriella thanked him and said that she would be eternally grateful to him before hanging up. She began packing her things.

She went to the Samantha and Moira's room. They both welcomed her with open arms. After hugging, Gabriella put her clothes in one of the empty bureau drawers that Moira had saved for any guests that she might have had; and then Gabriella sat on one of the chairs that Moira had in her room. She said that she was exhausted and needed to lie down. Moira pointed to the vacant cot that she also used for guests and told her that the cot was all hers and that she and Samantha were going to the coffee shop. When they left, Gabriella breathed a sigh of relief and went to what now was her bed. She went to sleep almost immediately.

The next day, Gabriella thought that it would be a good idea if the two girls and she entered into a pact that focused on being friends for life. She woke up the other girls and told them of her idea. They thought that it was a great idea. Gabriella went through her things and found a small knife that they could use to draw blood from their middle finger. They gathered in a circle, cut their fingers and, after exchanging the blood in their little fingers, promised to be loyal to one another for life.

Meanwhile, Cappy was still intent on his investigation and his obsession with the earring drove him half crazy. He wished that the obsession would leave him but he was convinced that it had something to do with the murder. What? He didn't know. Soon it became clear to him that the earring was only incidental and the two suspects that he should have been looking at were Iota and Sparks. Iota was in the men's room at the time of the shooting and Sparks was the one who had given the victim mouth-to-mouth resuscitation, but he was in the men's room before all of those people came. He paused and thought some more. Iota and Sparks! He should speak to them again.

He left his desk and all the paper work that was there. He went back to his car and headed for Savan. Meanwhile, Iota, bothered by the murder of Shaw, which he had committed, was beginning to act strangely looking at his roommates and giving them threatening stares. He also said that he was next to God in all of the things that he did, whether he intended to act or whether he intended to not act. It didn't make any difference. He had the power to let other people live or die. He was able to let them live or to take their lives away from them. He said that when things go wrong, he was the one who was responsible.

Both Galvin and Sparks were visibly upset with what Iota was saying and they both tried to calm him down. Sparks thought of the black cat that he and Gabriella had seen and thought for a moment that it had significance. It must, he thought. But the immediate problem was Iota and what to do about his ravings. Just then there was a knock on their dormitory door and when they asked who was there, Cappy announced himself. He wasn't concerned with Galvin, just Iota and Sparks. Galvin let him in when he recognized Cappy's voice.

"Good day detective. How are you?"

"I'm well. You guys are well?"

Cappy was intent on talking to both Iota and Sparks and he told Galvin to go to the coffee shop. Galvin complied but didn't like being told what to do. He nonetheless put on his jacket and left the room. He headed over to the coffee shop. Moira, Samantha and Gabriella were there having coffee when he arrived. Galvin smiled at them before he ordered a cup of coffee himself. But he was still fuming at Cappy telling him to go to the coffee shop. He didn't like being told what to do. Like most college students, he favored his independence. When he got his coffee, he went to the table and sat next to Roger French and Charles Richards. He said hello but he also said that he wasn't in the mood for any chit chat. He simply wanted to have a cup of coffee. They both respected his wishes; they didn't speak to him at all. They resumed eating and drinking their coffee. They were having sandwiches too with their coffee.

While Galvin was sitting in the coffee shop, Cappy was talking to both Sparks and Iota about the murder. He thought that they both were a bit strange and he attributed their strangeness to their being college students. College students he thought were in a world of their own and were not privy to all the burdens that there were in life. Perhaps this explained partying and drinking which were plagues at all universities and colleges, he thought.

He wanted to speak to both of them, but only one at a time. He asked Iota if he would mind waiting outside when he spoke to Sparks. Iota complained that he was always left out of things. He told Cappy that he had every right to listen to what Sparks had to say about the murder and that maybe he could be of help to Cappy in interpreting what Sparks was saying about the murder. But if Cappy insisted, he would wait outside in the hallway. He said that he hadn't said his prayers to himself yet. Waiting in the hallway would give him the opportunity to do that. Cappy thought that it was an odd thing for him to say. He smiled at Iota when he finally left the room. Both he and Sparks looked at one another as he left. Their looks were curious. Sparks made the comment that Iota was a strange dude but that he was not always like that. Just from the murder, he thought and he told Cappy that.

Cappy just shrugged his shoulders and began the interview. He asked Sparks what he was doing the night of the murder. Sparks said that he was just drinking from the punch bowl when Long asked him to see what could be keeping Shaw and Iota in the men's room. Sparks said that he didn't like being told what to do or how to act by anyone, least of all by Long. But he complied. He said that he went to the men's room and saw the body of Shaw lying on the floor. There was blood everywhere, he said. He told Cappy that he began to apply mouth-to-mouth resuscitation immediately while Iota just stood there. He had learned about this method in his health class and he thought that by doing it, he would save Shaw. When Cappy asked him if he was sure about what he had told him about Shaw and Iota, Sparks said that he was. Cappy thought that it was odd that Sparks had given Shaw mouth-to-mouth while Iota just stood there. Sparks told Cappy that he screamed for someone to call security or the police. That's when Long came into the room. Long was the one who called the police he said. Long also called security. When security came, they felt that it was a police matter, so Long or security called the police. He told Cappy all this while Iota waited outside. Cappy thought that he should interview Sparks again. He was still suspicious about him and he thought that he might have had a motive for killing Shaw. Perhaps he was jealous of Shaw for some reason or another. But he would have to wait. Now he had to turn his attention to Iota. He excused Sparks and suggested that he go to the coffee shop. He called Iota in.

Iota was standing alone in the hallway. At first he couldn't believe that the interview with Sparks took so long. But when Cappy called him in, he thought differently. His thought now was to convince Cappy that he nothing to do with the killing. What should he say? He thought that he shouldn't say much. He thought that the least he said the better for him. He could deny everything and simply say that he was in the men's room to go to the bathroom when a shot rang out from outside the window and Shaw was hit. Afterwards, he ran to the window and saw Lane there. Cappy would believe what he told him; the Boston police are not that smart he thought. Even though Lane was acquitted of the crime, he felt that by focusing upon him would take away any suspicion that Cappy, or anyone else had about the murder. He told Cappy what his feelings were about Lane. Cappy was skeptical about what Iota had told him, but his job was to conduct interviews with everyone involved and not to make any judgments about suspects of the crime. After his talk with Iota, when he was satisfied that he had covered all of the material that he wanted to, Cappy said "thanks" to him, and then his thoughts were on proceeding to go home to his wife and to the twins. He thought that he was a lucky man to have such a beautiful wife and such great kids.

Before heading home, he stopped at his office. His men were fooling around, but they stopped when they saw him. Without saying a word, he went to his desk and proceeded to look at the papers that were piled on his desk; the pile grew from the last time he looked at the papers that he had. His captain called him over when he saw him and asked him about the interviews that he had conducted. He told the captain about what Sparks and Iota had told him and said that he still had his doubts about their guilt or innocence. He said that Iota looked rather strange compared to Sparks and that he had said things that led Cappy to focus more on him.

Meanwhile, both Sparks and Iota were discussing the visit that Cappy had made to their dorm room. They had gone to the coffee shop and took a table in the corner where nobody could hear them. They both thought that they were suspects in the murder. Sparks denied any involvement in it and Iota said that he was not involved either. They both awaited the opportunity to talk with Cappy again. Iota began to talk strangely. He again claimed that he had the power to change people's lives. The more he talked, claiming to be Godlike, the more frightened Sparks became.

Sparks thought that it might be a wise thing to call Cappy and tell him what Iota had said. He told Iota that he was going to the bathroom down the hall, but when he left the room he went immediately to the payphone and placed a call to the Boston Police and asked for Cappy.

"Hello, Mr. Longquist. This is Barry Sparks. Listen, I think you should know that Mark Iota is talking like a nut. He scares me. You had better speak to him again. He really scares me."

"Why? What does he say?"

"He claims that he is like God and has the power to change people."

"Ok, I'll talk to him."

Cappy hung up the phone and was concerned about what Sparks had told him. He was very concerned. He thought that he had better talk with Iota again. Once again, he picked up the phone from its cradle and he placed a call to Savan and asked to speak to Lane, the Dean of Discipline, who had just been acquitted of the murder. When Lane got on the phone, Cappy asked him about Iota and told him that he was acting strangely. He told Lane that he was worried about him and that the more strangely he acted the more he was concerned about the safety of Barry Sparks. He also said that he was now convinced that Sparks was innocent of the crime and that Mark Iota was probably the guilty one. Lane said that he would call Sparks in and talk to him.

When they were finished with their conversation, Cappy was more convinced than ever that Iota was the guilty one. His conviction of Iota's involvement in the murder led him to go back to Saven to arrest him. He went to his room and told him that he was under arrest. Iota, of course, protested by first saying that he hadn't done anything wrong and then saying that he would sue the Boston Police for this affront. When Cappy put handcuffs on him and gave him the "Miranda ruling", he led him out of his dormitory. All the students they saw were shocked at the sight of Iota in handcuffs. Sometimes students hang out on the steps of their dormitories. That is a tradition at Savan and other colleges. When the students that were hanging on the steps after Cappy had given Iota the "Miranda" warning and put him in handcuffs, they began to groan at what they were watching, and then the groans turned to teasing Iota for being in handcuffs and the circumstance that he was in. Of course, they didn't understand that he was being arrested for Shaw's murder. They began to cheer the Boston police as Cappy placed him in his police cruiser. Then he drove back to the police headquarters.

While all this was going in, Tell was in his office still trying to cut the size of his current list of clients. Of course, he was the one who defended Lane at his trial. Lane's name was still on the list but he decided that he would omit it when he first picked up the list. His goal was to trim the list as much as he could before doing anything else. When he saw Lane's name on it, he immediately took his name off.

Just then the phone rang. It was Cappy. After they exchanged formal greetings, he asked Cappy why he had called. Cappy told him that he had to arrest Iota for the murder at Savan and thought that Tell should be informed of this. He suggested that Tell probably would be his defense lawyer. Tell, after thinking about this for some time, agreed. After all, Tell was familiar enough with the case having defended Lane. He immediately began to plot his strategy.

Meanwhile, Iota was in a holding cell at the police station. He began to grumble that he had the power to eliminate the entire police department if he wanted to. The guard told him to be quiet but he persisted. Finally, the guard yelled at him through the bars of his cell. The guard yelled at him furiously. Finally, Iota shut up about his "power". The guard was the one who took him into the courtroom where Judge Haley was presiding. Haley, after Tell had said that Iota was a student at Savan and was not a flight risk, set the bail amount at $125,000 which Iota's father met. Iota, now released from his holding cell went to see the guys that he used to hang out with on the corner of the street where he lived. He used to "hang out" with them before he was accepted at Savan. They all had strange nicknames like "Squeaky", "Snowshoes" and "Superman."

Iota was from Charlestown, the same town that Cappy was from but on a different street. He didn't have too far to go when he left the guys on the corner to get to Savan. He certainly did not need anything. When he arrived at his home, his father who had put up the bail money asked him if he had anything to do with the murder. He confided to his dad that he taken one of the guns from the display case that his dad had. He also took bullets so that he could impress his classmates at Savan. When Shaw told him that he had a girlfriend and teased him and showed him the earring he got mad. Then Shaw said that he that he had a relation with another woman. Iota got furious, pulled out the gun and shot him.

Chapter Nineteen

His father was comfortable with Mark's homosexuality, but murder was another thing. How could he be involved in any way with a murder? He yelled at Mark and begged him to tell him that it was not true, any of it. His dad was a widower and spent his days brooding about the loss of his wife. He was healthy enough but a widower nonetheless. The only thing that gave him any surcease from the loss of his wife was his gun collection. He kept saying why, why? Why did he lose his wife and why did Iota take the gun from his display case and use it to murder another human being? He simply couldn't understand it.

Muldoon meanwhile was attending to his own affairs. He had gone home to his house in West Roxbury where he lived with his father. His mother had died last year and his dad was drinking heavily. He was an alcoholic. When Sean came home and saw the condition his father was in, he thought that it would be a good idea for both of them to go to an AA meeting at Saint Mary's. They had meetings there every night. After arguing with his father about whether a meeting was called for, they finally agreed and called a cab to take them to the church.

The church was located in the North End of Boston and its hall was used for Alcoholics Anonymous meetings. Saint Mary's had meetings every night and on Saturday mornings. When they got there Muldoon's father, Neil, was getting to be a bit sober when the meeting began. But he still had the effects of heavy drinking. He had been drinking all day.

He knew many of the people who were there. He greeted them with a smile and a brief hello as both he and Sean took a seat in the back of the room. When the meeting started and the principle speaker was introduced, the room was quiet again excepting for a fan that blew cold air around. The speaker gave his first name and said that he was an alcoholic. That is what the first step of the program suggests. A speaker who wants to talk and share his story with the attendees must follow this rule. He said that he had been drinking since he was very young. He also related a story that he had heard from others in the program; it seems that a man, not him, was going to a meeting but before he got to the meeting he had two drinks. "A bird in the bush is better than two in your hand." Everybody laughed at this pun.

After he spoke, the floor was open for any questions that the audience might have. Sean Muldoon was tempted to say something but he remained silent. His father's eyes were getting droopy. Somebody from the back of the room, near Sean and his dad, said that he identified with what the speaker had said, particularly with the story about the man who had two drinks before going to a meeting. He called it a "slip." Other members of the group chimed in saying that they too agreed with the man in the rear of the room that it was a "slip."

Muldoon and his father left the meeting after the group held hands and said the Our Father. Sean hailed a cab. The cab took them home to West Roxbury. In the cab they talked about the meeting. Sean's father was getting more and more sober as the cab headed for West Roxbury, and he said that he was glad that Sean had insisted that they go to the meeting at Saint Mary's. He always liked that meeting he said to Sean. They both were tired and went to bed as soon as they got home. Sean could not sleep, however, and went down to the kitchen and poured himself a glass of milk and got a cookie to eat. He always had problems with sleeping. He put on the small television set that was in the kitchen and watched the news. The news broadcast was the first time that he heard that Iota got arrested for the murder at Savan. He was surprised at this announcement about Iota being arrested and he exclaimed "wow" when he heard the news. Some things do surprise us. And some things we take for granted.

Sean Muldoon woke the next morning after a fitful sleep. He had his usual cup of coffee and went to work. When he got there Cappy was waiting for him. Cappy had gotten to work early, but was still a bit under the weather with his illness. He had taken the advice of Pat and called the doctor for an appointment. His appointment was for the afternoon. He told Muldoon that he had better take care of it and whatever interviews or other work that he still had on his desk. Muldoon agreed with him. When Cappy had finished the work that was on his desk, he left the room. Muldoon now had full responsibility for the remaining interviews.

Muldoon appeared confused. He looked at the desk and was amazed at all the paper work that was there. He said to himself that he had better get busy and take care of the pile that Cappy had begun to read. He was glad that Cappy had begun to read the paper work. Muldoon was not thrilled with paper work. Meanwhile Cappy was at the doctor's office. He had to wait, and he looked at a magazine which he perused while waiting. Finally, the nurse called his name and he went into the inner office and waited some more for the doctor. When the doctor came in and asked

Cappy what the problem was, Cappy told him that he was not feeling well the past couple of days. The doctor told him to undress so that he could examine him more fully.

Cappy obliged and the doctor proceeded with the examination. When he had finished, he had a stern look on his face as he told Cappy that he was sorry but that Cappy had an ulcer. The doctor told him that he was free to get another opinion but that he was certain of his diagnosis. He said that Cappy would have to be careful of what he ate, gets lots of rest, work less and stop worrying. Cappy reluctantly agreed to take better care of himself, but he still was focused on the murder and Iota. He knew that he was guilty. When he got dressed, he headed back to his office.

When he got there he told his captain what the doctor had said. The captain accepted the news without inquiring anything more from Cappy than he already told him. He told Cappy to go home to Charlestown. He asked Cappy to select one of his three men to take control of the murder at Savan. Cappy thought that Muldoon would do the job well. He would be the one to continue the investigation. After all, he was the person who knew the suspects and he was the one who took notes on the interviews that Cappy had done. The captain agreed.

Cappy left the office to go home. He was glad that the captain had agreed with his choice of Muldoon to continue the investigation. Muldoon was more knowledgeable than the other guys he thought and would do a fine job. The only problem that he saw was to convince Muldoon that he should be the one to take over the investigation. After all, he was in his first year as a member of the Boston Police and might do badly. But someone had to take Cappy's place and Muldoon was the logical candidate.

Meanwhile, Tell was in his office going over the cases that he had. He focused on the Lane case. He was still fascinated with the murder at Savan and with Lane. He thought that his defense of Lane was effective. Lane got off despite the complaint that he took out against his wife, Lisa. Just then the phone rang and Tell picked it up. It was the father of Iota that was calling. After they exchanged pleasantries, they got down to business. Mr. Iota wanted Tell to defend his son. Tell agreed under the condition that nobody would interfere with his defense. Mr. Iota agreed and said that as far as he was concerned, Tell would have absolute control over his son's defense.

Tell, when he put the phone down, took a piece of paper and began to write down his strategies. He thought of a number of things. Should he say that Mark Iota was not sane when he committed the crime?

Should he say, in his opening remarks, that Mark was sane but that he only acted in self-defense in killing Shaw? He continued to take both ideas into consideration as he sat there and thought about the murder at Savan.

Mark Iota, when he was in custody, acted strangely. The guard continued to be concerned about his behavior but simply shrugged his shoulders when Mark said anything that the guard thought was unusual. Mark was behaving oddly and claimed that he was God and could control people's lives, even the guard's. The guard continued to ignore him. He wished that he was home with his wife and kids and enjoying himself with the television game between Boston and New York. But the reality was that he was assigned to guard the one who was suspected of killing Robert Shaw at Savan College.

And we should live within reality.

CHAPTER TWENTY

Muldoon was concerned when he heard that Cappy had an ulcer and had selected him to take his place. The captain had called him in his office and explained to Muldoon that he was the logical one to replace Cappy since he was the one who took notes during the interviews. Muldoon, aware that he was only in his first year, was very concerned about his abilities to conduct an investigation. He was comfortable enough to record what people had said to Cappy, but conducting the rest of the investigation was another story. Of course, all the interviews were conducted and there was little else to do other than to focus on the trial of Iota and to take care of the other parts of the investigation. He was determined to do what the captain had told him to do.

After he left the captains office, he went immediately to the phone and called his father to tell him the news. He explained to his dad what the captain had said and that he was intent to do what the captain had expected of him. He then called Cappy and said that he was sorry that Cappy was ill but that he would handle things and that Cappy should get as much rest as possible. When he hung up the phone it began to dawn on him that he was really in charge of the investigation. He said "wow" to himself and that he should get himself and his two men ready to resume where they had left off. He had every assumption that the two men who had been with Cappy since the inception of the investigation would now work for him. Both men had already spoken to the captain and they both accepted what the captain had told them. They both said that they were willing to work with and take orders from a first year man. When the captain spoke with them they both agreed. Both were long time members of the Boston police department. Their names were Ethan Frane and Michael Sullivan.

Muldoon was concerned about leading the investigation. He was particularly concerned being a first year man leading men who were on the police force for a long time. But he was intent on doing the job that the captain had laid out for him. He thought about the fact that Iota had been charged with the murder at Savan as he heard on the news that he watched in his kitchen. He thought that Iota was strange. He thought this way about Iota ever since he recorded the interview with him that Cappy had conducted.

Meanwhile, Tell was still in his office. He was trying to determine what he would say in his opening remarks to the jury. It was critical for him to do a good job. Juries are funny; they often are offended when a lawyer does a bad job with the opening remarks. Sometimes it makes the difference between finding the defendant guilty or innocent. Tell was aware of this as he practiced his opening remarks. He was engrossed in thought when his phone rang. It was Iota's father. He appeared to sound terribly concerned to Tell. He explained to Tell that his son was acting strangely and he thought that Tell should be aware of this. When Tell asked Iota's father if he wanted to use the insanity defense, the father after thinking for a minute or two, said that he did not want Tell to do that. He said that Tell should plead not guilty to the charge of murder that his son faced. He really thought that his son may have been justified in what he had done. The fact that Iota's father thought this way made Tell's job easier in preparing what he would say to the jury.

Tell hung up the phone and went back to preparing what he would say to the jury in his opening remarks. He looked around his office. One could tell he was nervous when he did. For all of the adulation that he commanded, he was not in control of his emotions. He began to write down what he would say to the jury in his opening remarks. He wrote fast. He seemed to always be in a hurry. He wrote something about his personal life and what he would say about Iota to the jury. He was brought up in Chelsea by his aunt and spent several years in the military before attending Savan and then law school. He had quite a personal background.

He knew that Iota's dad had wanted him to plead not guilty instead of using a mental illness defense. Although he thought that the mental illness approach would be a better and more effective technique if he was to be found not guilty. He also recognized that the father of Iota was paying the bills; and he who pays must always rule. This is true in any business arrangement whether one is talking about the commercial world or the legal field.

When he finished writing, he continued to practice by walking around the office and gesturing the way that he would in court. He always did this before a big trial and he knew that the press and the media would be all over the trial about the murder at Savan. The press had already written at least a few stories about it and it was the subject of frequent news analysis.

At last the preparation was finished. He sat down in his chair exhausted from his labor. He thought that he had better go get a drink at the bar, The Guild and Feather, where all of the other lawyers hung out.

The Guild and Feather was a rather old barroom. It had an air about it that was rather unusual. The large bar was not the kind that you would ordinarily find. It was very lavish with artificial flowers in pots hanging from the ceiling over the bar and it was flooded with small roses. There were couches strewn around the bar area where patrons could relax after a hard day's work.

Tell got into his car and drove there. His car was a small one. Often he thought that he should buy a bigger one but now was not the time. He arrived at the bar and he saw a number of his friends and a number of his enemies too, especially Jack Burns who would be the one prosecuting the case against his client Mark Iota. He went over to the bar and sat beside Burns. Burns looked up from his drink and seeing Tell offered him his greeting. Tell responded by simply saying hello. You could tell both Burns and Tell were uncomfortable by simply looking at them.

After talking about the weather and other more mundane things, their conversation turned to the murder at Savan. This was Tell's intention. He wanted to talk to somebody about it especially after all of the effort he put into his preparation back in his office about what he would say to the jury.

Seeing Burns at the bar was a bonus. Burns introduced the topic of the murder at Savan by asking Tell what he thought about it. Tell said that he couldn't talk about it because it would violate the law that forbade opposing lawyers to talk about cases that they were involved with. Burns looked directly at him and said that despite the law, he had something that he wanted to say. He told Tell that he would beat him when the trial began. Lawyers aren't supposed to say things like that. The law forbade that too. But he wanted to prod Burns into saying something like that; it was Tell's intention in the first place regardless of the law. One could tell that Burns had been taken in by the trap. Tell had wanted him to say that he, Burns, would say that he would beat him. When and if Tell had won in the trial, he would laud it over Burns for a long time. At least this was his plan.

Sometimes we all do the same thing especially when money is involved or when business deals are at stake. Sometimes we all make errors that figuratively come up and haunt us.

Tell ordered a drink from the bartender. He called the bartender over to where he was seated at the bar and he asked him to give him a scotch and soda that he gulped down as soon as he got it from the bartender. When he did gulp it down, he looked at Burns and said that he had better get home. He didn't live far from The Guild and Feather. He got into his car and drove it home. He lived at one of the condos at

Commonwealth Avenue by himself. When he got there he changed his clothes putting something more comfortable on.

Then he rehearsed again what he would say to the jury in his opening remarks.

CHAPTER TWENTY ONE

Tell was not sure what he would say to the jury. After thinking for a long time, he again thought that it would be a good idea for him to begin with something personal about his life, and then talk about why Iota had pled not guilty. He enjoyed trials that were held with a jury. He was a very conceited man. When he had finished with his rehearsal he went into his bedroom to lie down. He thought that he saw a shadow there. A man was waiting for him.

The man was Mr. Iota. After Tell had registered shock at seeing a man in his bedroom, he found the courage to ask Mr. Iota what he was doing in his bedroom. Mr. Iota told him that he was sorry that they had to meet this way, but he was concerned about the plea that Tell would enter. Tell remained shocked at the whole scene. Tell told Mr. Iota how he felt. He also assured him that he would enter a plea of not guilty by reason of mental incompetence that he had already suggested. Underneath, he felt that making a plea of mental incompetence would be a better route for him to go since a plea of mental incompetence would mean, if one was to be found guilty, that the person involved would be looked at as a patient rather than a convict. Either way you win. If the person is found guilty, he is hospitalized. If he is found not guilty, he walks.

Mr. Iota explained to Tell that the door was not locked when he came to see him. He had wanted to take one of his guns with him but decided not to. He told Tell that he knocked on the door several times and when nobody answered he tried the door and it opened. He looked around the apartment before creeping into Tell's bedroom. Tell was furious when he saw Mr. Iota standing there. He told him that he must be kidding. He had thoughts of when he was a kid and someone broke into his home and went to his bedroom. It reminded him of that time and the person who broke into his home that was known by the entire neighborhood as a gay person. Tell told Mr. Iota that he was not gay if that was on Mr. Iota's mind. Mr. Iota laughed at this suggestion and said that even though his son was gay, it did not mean that he was. Being gay was not a matter of genetics but rather it was the result of learned behavior. Being gay to him was not a condition that anyone should take lightly however. A gay person, he said, was apt to do something of a sexual nature that others did not approve of. In addition, the people who felt this way were shocked because the same family circumstances that were related to him being gay were not found in siblings who were straight. To him, it was all a matter of the environment. While he admitted the influence of heredity, he said that other factors should be taken in consideration as well. On the other hand, Tell thought that being gay had more to do with heredity than to the environment. But at the moment, he was more interested in why Iota had found it necessary to break into his apartment rather than coming to his office and discussing the trial with him. He expressed the anger and rage that he was feeling to Mr. Iota.

Mr. Iota took a long pause in his breathing and said to Tell that he was sorry that he had broken into his apartment and that Tell had found him in his bedroom. He said that he was not homosexual. He was straight when it came to sexual orientation. He said that he and his late wife always had a good relationship. He insisted that he was not gay.

Tell smiled and said that he forgave Mr. Iota for the intrusion into his home. He invited him into his living room. Mr. Iota took a seat after saying that he had no objection to gay people getting married. He said that love should be the only thing that mattered. He spouted that if two people loved one another, truly did love one another and understood what love was all about, then that should be sufficient whether talking about a straight person or a person who was gay. Iota took a seat on the coach across from Tell who sat in an easy chair. Tell opened the conversation by repeating that he forgave Mr. Iota for barging in the way that he did. He insisted that he still didn't understand why Mr. Iota didn't go to his office to discuss the plea deal. He said that he still felt that by offering a not guilty plea when he faced the jury was a better way to go rather than an insanity plea. Mr. Iota, despite his initial feeling that he wanted Tell to accept the insanity plea, finally agreed.

When there was nothing left to say, Tell escorted Mr. Iota to the door and said goodnight. He said to himself that he was glad that it was over. Now he was free to concentrate on what he would say to the jury in his opening remarks. After thinking for a while, he agreed with his initial thought of saying something about his own upbringing and then saying something about Iota being not guilty. He was pleased with himself.

Muldoon in the meantime was aware that both he and Cappy had completed the interviews. He was also aware that Iota was arrested and arraigned for the murder at Savan College. He thought that Iota was guilty but could say nothing. He was not sure of Tell's plea arrangement but, nonetheless, he didn't feel that there was anything that Tell could say that would cause him to change his mind.

Back in his office, Tell continued to work on his opening remarks to the jury. He still thought that it was a pretty good plan to focus on his own upbringing before he made comments about Iota and his plea of not guilty. He was adamant about not focusing on a plea of not guilty by reason of mental illness. He began to write.

"Ladies and gentlemen of the jury, let me tell you something about myself. I was born here in Boston in the Charlestown section. When I was a kid I shoveled snow in the winter before working delivering orders for a local grocery store. When I was older, I served in the navy while working nights at a gas station. When I got out of the navy, I went back to Savan College for my degree while working nights at The Boston Globe. So I worked hard all my life. Later, I went to law school after a friend had recommended that I do. I do law now, that's what I do, I do it for a living. I defend people who are innocent of the crime that they have been charged with and I know that they are innocent. Otherwise, I would not defend them.

"So, I have worked all my life. Sometimes, the jobs that I had were terribly boring sometime not. At least I tried.

"It's the same today though. I am defending a man who is not guilty of any crime. Unfortunately, he was at the wrong place at the wrong time. Somebody else committed the murder at Savan!

"Thank you for your attention."

"That should do the trick," he said to himself.

With that, he put his pen and paper down. He was tired from the busy day that he had, particularly when he found a stranger in his bedroom. Mr. Iota had shaken him up. He would write down his defense of Iota at another time. Now he was tired. He went into his bedroom, got into his bed and fell asleep almost immediately.

The next day Tell wrote the second part of his what he considered to be his masterpiece. He began by saying that he considered Iota innocent. He wrote it down on the pad that he was using. He wrote:

"Members of the jury, I will prove my client's innocence to you. Iota was a friend of Robert Shaw's, the boy who was murdered that dreadful night at Savan. I am sure that someone else was there and shot Shaw and then threw the gun out the window. Is it possible that Iota saw this unknown person?

"I will show you that Iota not only knew this person, but that he spoke to this person after Shaw was shot.

"It is no accident that a girl committed suicide when she went home to Connecticut. She said that she was accosted on the train by some unknown man and that was the reason that she was stressed. But why would a young lady commit suicide over this? Wasn't there another reason? Surely most women do not commit suicide simply because they might have been accosted. There must be another reason for this girl to take her own life.

"Her name was Megan Sullivan. I will submit to you that many young ladies came into the men's room after Shaw was shot. In all that confusion, is it possible that Sullivan hid in one of the stalls until Shaw came into the men's room, knowing that he would have to use the men's room eventually? Then, after she shot Shaw and threw the gun out the window, might she have mingled with the crowd that came into the restroom? After all, the crowd had a great deal of female students who came into the men's room. Not only were there men there, there were women too!

"And Megan was quite drunk and she had made a date with Shaw to take her to the dance that evening. Shaw apparently had one of her earrings in his pocket and probably was showing off about it to Iota.

"I will show you, members of the jury, all of this while my client sits very close to you.

"Thank you for listening to me."

Tell was pleased with what he had written down on the pad. He knew that the jury would only need one person to find Iota not guilty. And he took advantage of that piece of the law in writing down his remarks to the jury by using the question of possibility on them. But today he was going to have a drink, maybe more than one. To him this mode of celebration was always called for when he completed what he would say to the jury. So he went back to The Guild and Feather. The crowd had changed since he was there with Jack Burns. There were more women sitting around the bar at the Guild and Feather than men, and they were all young and beautiful. That was not unusual for an evening; most bars have more women than men in the evening. And they all consider themselves young and beautiful.

Both men and women were dancing to the music, or should they be characterized as just jumping up and down. This was the ordinary way to dance.

Tell was an older man and was not by no means beautiful, nor handsome. He went up to the bar where there was a vacant seat. He looked around the bar and was tempted to say something to the girl sitting beside him. Instead he ordered a drink from the bartender. He generally ordered scotch and water but today for some reason or another he ordered Grey Goose Vodka and tonic. With the liquid courage that he had from gulping the cool drink down he began to speak. The girl sitting beside him was a young girl. Her name was Deirdre. In her eyes he was an old man. Like older men he was not aware that she considered him to be old; he considered himself to be a younger man than he actually was. But he did want to say something to her and begin a conversation. She was quite beautiful. He took a long drink from the glass and turned to her and introduced himself. He was very self-conscious.

"Hi, my name is William Tell."

"That's nice."

"I'm a lawyer."

"That's nice."

"I guess that you don't want to talk." What a way to start a conversation he thought.

"I don't mean to be rude, But I am waiting for someone," she said.

She then told Tell her name when he asked her and she said that she knew Samantha Lavine at Savan. She also knew Megan Sullivan. When Tell asked her about the suicide that the Sullivan girl had committed, Deirdre became very flushed. She had worked in education as a teacher and she said that she really didn't want to talk about the suicide. She said that it was too painful. Tell, trying not to be insistent, said that the whole thing was a tragedy. He was then silent, but underneath he had different thoughts. He wanted to say that he felt that she was responsible for her suicide and as such she had obligations for committing that act. Perhaps, he thought, he might even pin the murder on her! Maybe she was indeed the guilty party! She could have been waiting in a stall for him to come into the men's room. Farfetched? Perhaps. But what lawyer ever objected to something that others might define as farfetched?

Underneath, he planned to bring the girl who committed suicide into what he would say to the jury. Somebody had to be blamed for the murder at Savan. To refer to anybody who committed suicide was a good plan, he thought. He looked at Deirdre with a subtle and silent smile on his face and he told her that he felt sorry for Megan's friends and especially for her family. He excused himself and said that he had to get back to work and that it was pleasant to have talked with her. Then he left the bar. With his now potential ammunition about Megan Sullivan, he felt confident that the jury would be impressed with the notion that Megan might have been the guilty party who was responsible for Shaw's murder. After all, it only took one member of the jury to cast a doubt about the guilt or innocence of the defendant.

To Tell that was enough. She was the one who made a date with Shaw to take her to the dance. He must have been the one who took her earring from her room. She had the other earring in her possession. She could have been waiting in one of the stalls; waiting for him to answer the call of nature. She could have been there with a gun. Guns were a part of her family's inheritance. Her father had an extensive collection of guns in the display case his office. It was all possible, he thought. All that Tell had to do was to mention the suicide during the trial, the guns and say that she could have been her waiting in one of the stalls for him. It surely would be enough to convince someone that his client may not be guilty, he thought. She could have been waiting for him in a stall armed with a gun. Anything was possible. All he had to do was to find a member of the jury to convince; someone who was gullible enough to believe that she might have been there.

When the day of jury selection came Tell was ready. He knew the kind of person that he wanted to be included as a jury member. Basically, he was looking for somebody who was gullible. He spotted one man immediately. The man was a middle aged man, who was a carpenter. His name was Fred Scott. He had responded to one of the questions about whether he thought a man could be guilty of a crime while at the same time be innocent by reason of not knowing the difference between right and wrong. When he had answered yes to this question, after thinking about it for a long time, Tell immediately said that he had no objection to him as a member of the jury. Tell thought that he had found just the man that he wanted; someone who would insist to the other members of the jury that the defendant was not guilty.

Meanwhile, Muldoon was still pondering how he would conduct the investigation further. He thought that he should go to the Sullivan family and speak to the mother about Megan's suicide. It is always difficult to speak to a member of a suicide victim's family or to anybody in the family of a dead person, but he felt it was necessary for him to speak to the mother. After getting on the train to Connecticut, he felt more comfortable about his decision to go. He felt comfortable because this was the right thing to do, he thought. That is, until he got to the front door of Megan's house. Then he began to have a panic attack. Perhaps he should have started with Mrs. Spinoza. Maybe he could have started with Mr. Sullivan, Megan's dad. But here he was.

He rang the doorbell and Mrs. Sullivan answered. She was a tall lady with blondish hair that hangs over her unblemished face, despite what she had been through with the suicide of her daughter; she still looked beautiful to Muldoon. She asked him what he wanted.

"Good day, mam. I'm Sean Muldoon, Clyde Longquist's assistant. Mr. Longquist is not feeling well and I am the leader of the investigation into the murder that happened at Savan College. I have come to ask you some questions," Muldoon said sheepishly.

CHAPTER TWENTY TWO

Mrs. Sullivan stared at Muldoon. You could tell by the expression on her face that she had that she was very, very upset. At first she resisted any questions but eventually she softened and invited Muldoon into her home. He accepted her invitation and he entered her home. She offered him a seat near the window and she sat down herself. He wondered how she would respond to his questions. He finally got enough courage and began by asking her something about Megan's childhood.

"Could you tell me something about Megan and what she did as a child?"

"She was such a beautiful child. Why did she do what she did? Why, why!" She was obviously very distressed at Megan taking her own life. She thought that she had better not say anything about the suicide until Mr. Sullivan came home. Just then the doorbell rang. It was Mrs. Spinoza.

Mrs. Spinoza sat down in one of the easy chairs that the Sullivan's had in their living room. After refusing a glass of wine offered by Mrs. Sullivan, she said that she felt so badly that Megan had taken her own life, that she had committed suicide. She tried to smile when she said that but a smile is very difficult when you are dealing with any family or family member where a loved one is lost for whatever reason. Finally, Muldoon spoke. He said that he also was very sorry about Megan but he had some questions about Megan and her taking her own life. He took out his yellow pad and began writing.

"Did you feel that Megan was upset about anything?" he directed this question at Mrs. Sullivan.

"No," she answered curtly.

"Nothing at all?"

"Well, she was concerned with the shooting at Savan."

'I see. Is there anything else that she might have been bothered by?"

"Nothing I can think of."

"Well thanks for your time." He was anxious to go.

With that, he left the room and the house while saying to himself that he was glad it was her and that it wasn't him; he was also glad that the interview with Mrs. Sullivan was over. But could it shed another light on the murder. Could it be that Megan had waited in one of the stalls and when Shaw came into the men's room, she erupted with emotion, shot him and then she threw the gun out the window? If so, it certainly would change the dynamics of his investigation.

When he got back to the office, the two men who were assigned to him were waiting for him while they took advantage of the break in the investigation by catching up on their paper work. After they greeted him, Muldoon went into the captain's office. He told the captain about his meeting with Mrs. Sullivan and his new theory about the murder at Savan. Maybe Megan Sullivan was not as innocent as she appeared, he said to the captain. The captain, while he understood what Muldoon had said, shook his head in disagreement. Muldoon was also intent on what Cappy had thought about the earring. Muldoon knew that he was obsessive about it and wondered why.

"How did she know that Shaw would come into the men's room when he did?"

"I hadn't thought too much about that. I still have to make other determinations."

With that, he left the office with a shrug and a scowl on his face. He was upset at the captain's comment. But he was determined to follow through with his theory that Megan might have something to do with the murder at Savan, in fact she was the murderer!

He went over to his desk, the one that Cappy had used and picked up the phone. He wanted to call both the defense attorney Tell and the prosecutor, Ann Dunn. Tell was glad that the prosecutor was a woman.

First he called Ann Dunn. And he said to her that he was the chief investigator replacing Cappy Longquist who was ill and that he was happy that the prosecutor was a woman.

CHAPTER TWENTY THREE

The jury had been selected and all of the necessary formalities had been completed for the trial of Mark Iota. Tell felt confident that he would get an acquittal. He looked over to the jury box focusing on the carpenter, whose name was Scott. He reasoned that all that he had to do was to convince him that it was plausible that Megan Sullivan had hidden in one of the stalls the night of the murder. When Shaw entered she shot him. If he could convince the carpenter that it was a sound theory, then he felt confident that the verdict would go in the direction that he wanted.

Tell was pleased that Ann Dunn was the prosecutor but when he found out the judge's name, he was not so pleased. The judge was Arthur Ford who was involved in issuing many indictments in other criminal cases. To Tell, having him as judge in this case was a good thing. Ford had had an affair with Ms. Dunn. All of the lawyers knew about it. It was talked about in bars where the lawyers congregated, in their offices, and in the rooms at the courthouse where they met before trials. To Tell, it was good news because he could use the affair to control Dunn. He didn't like the term "blackmail" but, in effect, he was going to use blackmail in dealing with her when and if he had the need. He smiled to himself at the prospect. Tell felt that the judge should obviously recuse himself but he also thought that he could use the affair to his advantage.

Dunn was a beautiful young lady. She had long blonde hair and a very womanly figure. Ford, on the other hand, was an older man who did not have a handsome face or body, but Dunn was in love with him. She loved him eagerly. She would do anything for him. Tell knew this and was quite willing to take advantage of their relationship if the opportunity presented itself.

The trial began. Television was forbidden in the courtroom by the judge who looked very imposing in front of the rest of the court and the audience in the elevated position of his chair on the bench in addition to the black robes that he wore. Tell stood beside Mark Iota, his client, when the clerk called for people to stand up as the judge entered the room. Iota had been waiting patiently for the trial to begin and he was dressed in a suit, shirt and tie. After the judge sat down and ordered the rest of the court to sit down, he asked Tell and his client whether they plead guilty or innocent to the crime that Iota was accused of. When Tell indicated that his client is pleading not guilty to the crime of murder there was a smile on Dunn's face. She felt that this would be an easy case for her to win. She was glad that she was the prosecutor.

Tell asked the judge for permission to call his first witness, Steve Long. When he was sworn in and took the witness box, Tell approached him with numerous questions about the murder and whether he had been involved when Shaw went to the men's room. He said that Shaw had shown him an earring and said that he needed to go to the bathroom. He said that Iota had to go as well and ran after Shaw. When he realized that there had been a shooting, he ran to the rest room and saw Shaw lying on the ground and Iota standing beside him. Iota seemed to be in a state of shock he said. He also said that Sparks began to give Shaw mouth-to-mouth resuscitation. Sparks had learned the technique in his first health class that they took.

"So what you are saying is that Shaw went to the men's room after showing you the earring and that Iota had followed him? Are you sure that you saw Iota standing beside the body when Sparks gave Shaw mouth-to-mouth resuscitation?"

"Yes I am."

Dunn immediately objected saying that the question had been asked and answered. Judge Ford agreed and ruled in her favor. Tell smiled, it was a technique that Tell had used before.

Long answered the question about whether people objected to him giving orders to do this or that. He said that he was not aware of it.

"Relevance?" Dunn objected.

"I withdraw the question," Tell responded.

Tell said that he didn't have any more questions of this witness and Judge Ford asked Ann Dunn if she had any questions of Long. When she replied that she had no questions, Long was excused from the witness box. Tell then called Barry Sparks to the stand.

Just as he did, a clerk ran into the room and told the judge that President Kennedy had been assassinated. The judge turned ashen and let the rest of the court know and said that the trial would continue on the next week. He then went into his office and closed the door. He took off his robes and sat at his desk sobbing. He had known the President well. He had spent time with him at Hyannis on the Cape. Just then the door burst open and Ann Dunn came in with a blank look on her face.

"I am so very sorry. I know how close you were to him." She wiped away the tears that were flowing from her eyes as she hugged the judge.

Apparently, the man who had committed the crime of assassination of a President escaped from the depository building by suggesting to an officer who ran to investigate that he was on lunch break. Everyone who was involved in a later commission agreed that it was a remarkable shot from the window of the school book depository where the assassin had set himself up with a place to hold the rifle. The assassin shot three times. At least two of the bullets hit their target and killed the President who had planned to give an address to three groups of business people who had congregated at a nearby Dallas hotel. He never would address the members who had assembled there.

A secret service man jumped on the rear of the Presidential car as it sped down Dealey Plaza toward the Parkland Hospital. Luckily, Mrs. Kennedy was not hurt in the assassination. She attempted to revive the President who was mortally wounded before assisting the secret service man who jumped on the rear of the car. One of the bullets that pierced the President lodged in the throat of Governor Connally who was sitting in front of the President.

The assassin had fled the building and attempted to hide in a nearby theater. He killed an officer by the name of J. D. Trippit before he was apprehended and brought to the police station where he was arraigned on a murder charge. Previously, he had spent a considerable amount of time in Cuba and was seen in New York City handing out pamphlets that said "Hands of Cuba" according to witnesses who were interviewed later in the investigation of the assassination. This investigation was called the Warren Commission Report.

Ann Dunn continued to hug the judge as he remained seated in his chair. The tears would not stop for either one of them. Suddenly Judge Ford got up from his chair and put the news on the television which the state of Texas was generous enough to place in his office.

Walter Cronkite was at his desk giving the news of the assassination. He took off his glasses, looked up at the clock which said 1pm Texas time and he said that the President was pronounced dead at the Parkland Hospital. He looked very professional when he reported the death of the President of the United States while nothing could have prevented the judge and Ann from sobbing.

But they both realized that they had a trial to conduct. They went home to their respective condos; Ann to her condo and the judge to his. In a couple of days the trial of Mark Iota began again.

Tell looked at both Ann and the judge. He was curious about how they both reacted to the news of Kennedy's assassination. He knew that the judge was close to Kennedy and had visited him in Hyannis. The judge had even gone on a sailing trip with the President. Tell felt sorry for him and he also felt sorry for Ann because of her relationship with him. How could anyone want to kill a president anyhow? How could anybody be that stupid? How could anybody lack such patriotism? Was the person insane? He suspected that a number of conspiracy theories would develop too. How can people think the way that they do?

The trial began again in earnest with both sides smirking at one another. Tell felt that he had a strong case and Ann Dunn thought that she had all of the marbles.

Tell began by recalling his witness, Barry Sparks. He looked glassy-eyed when he took the stand after swearing that he would tell the truth. Tell began his inquiry by asking him if he had heard the shot. When Sparks said that he didn't hear anything, Tell asked him why he had gone to the men's room anyhow. Sparks said that he didn't have to go but went after Long had told him to. He said that Long had a reputation for telling peoples what to do. He said that people objected to being told what to do in order to comply with Long's wishes. But he went along with his order to go, and he found Shaw lying still with Iota standing beside him. He began to give Shaw mouth-to-mouth resuscitation. They had been taught how to do it in the first health class that he took. When he was asked whether he had seen the earring that Shaw was showing around and bragging about, he answered that he had not seen it.

Tell asked him a few more questions about his relationship with Shaw and then he said that he had no more questions. Judge Ford asked Dunn if the State had any questions and Dunn replied that the State accepted what Sparks had said and that she had no questions of the witness; that she was convinced that Sparks had given Shaw mouth-to-mouth resuscitation as he said and that she didn't want to bother the witness any more than what he had testified to. Sparks had appeared quite nervous when he had answered Tells questions and Dunn saw this. She was quite sympathetic to that reality. Judge Ford then excused the witness from the witness box.

Tell called his next witness. Bill Galvin looked upset as he took the witness stand. He had not slept the night before being called. He was nervous about being a witness. Tell began the questions by asking him his name. Galvin responded that his name was William J. Galvin. After this, the questions began in earnest. Tell asked him what his role was in the murder of Shaw. He responded that he had nothing to do with the murder at Savan. Then Tell asked him if he was involved in flooding Pierce's office. Dunn immediately objected citing relevance to the case. The judge agreed and upheld the objection. Tell said that he would withdraw his observation, but he felt that Galvin's participation in flooding the office was important. It indicated that Shaw was in control of the others, Galvin, Sparks and his roommate Long. Dunn accepted what Tell had said but that her objection still stood. The judge agreed. Tell shrugged his shoulders and went on with the questioning.

He asked Galvin what he thought about Shaw. Was he too demanding? Tell asked him while thinking that the question would be objected to. But it wasn't. Tell proceeded in his questioning of Galvin. When Galvin said that he had difficulty following Shaw's orders when he was engaged in the flooding of Pierce's office, Tell smiled at the judge thinking that the prior objection of Dunn that the judge had sustained was wrong. Galvin said that Shaw and Long had a bad reputation with him. They had difficulty also with Sparks and Iota. Tell looked over to where Iota was sitting and thought to himself that maybe Iota was not guilty. Mark Iota sat motionless and did not react to Tell who was looking directly at him.

Dunn stood up and approached the witness when the judge asked her if she had any questions. She asked him whether or not he considered Iota guilty. Tell immediately objected saying that the defendant had already pled not guilty and that Galvin was not an expert on who might be innocent and who might be guilty. Judge Ford sustained the objection.

The trial flowed in the way that Tell wanted it to. He objected when he thought it was necessary and remained silent when he didn't. Dunn remained silent until Tell called Mark Iota to the stand. This was not expected. She had thought that Tell would not call the one who was accused of the crime to the witness box. She petitioned the judge for a break in the proceedings and the judge said that the trial would take a break for two hours. Dunn was pleased that he had ruled as he did and thought that she should go into his office. Tell was intrigued when he saw her exiting the courtroom and heading in the direction of the judges office.

He looked at her exit from the courtroom and said simply, hmm.

CHAPTER TWENTY FOUR

D unn glided into the judge's office and locked the door. The judge was disrobing and looked surprised to see her. But he was happy that she had come to see him. She looked into his eyes and saw that they were red and bloodshot. She went over to the desk where he was seated and kissed him then she kissed both of his eyebrows. Suddenly he seized her and said that they should be very careful not to put the trial in difficulty. He said to Ann that she knew that he loved her, but that he would have to recuse himself and rule the case a mistrial if they continued. He was a moral man and recognized the obligations that he had as a sitting judge. She said that it was all right, it was ok, that she only was concerned about him. He smiled and said that they had better get back to their business recognizing that it would be difficult to proceed given the Kennedy assassination and their interest in one another. But he had to go on and act like nothing had happened, not the assassination, nor their feelings for one another. He was intent on acting professionally. They both agreed to this and exited his office.

Meanwhile, Tell and some of the other lawyers who were not involved in the case were talking in the lounge about Ford and Dunn. Tell was very concerned and said that the judge should have recused himself and call for another judge to take his place. He could have brought the issue up by himself in the court room, he said, but that would put his career as a lawyer in considerable jeopardy. It would be better for him to ignore the whole thing and to take advantage of the situation when he asked questions of witnesses. If things did not go his way and Iota was found guilty, he might bring it up then. The lawyers agreed with him and what he had said about Ford and Dunn. It would not be wise at this time, they thought. To a man, they felt this way. There was one woman present, so the proper thing to say is "to both male and female they felt this way." Right now, it was time for Tell to head back to the courtroom.

When Tell got back, he recalled Iota to the witness box. He knew that it was risky to call the person who was charged with the crime, but it was a risk that he was willing to take. Dunn was shocked that he would do this and thought that it was a trap. He asked him directly if he was guilty or innocent. Iota replied that he was innocent and that there must have been someone else in the men's room or that someone could have been standing outside the men's room with a gun and fired it. After all, the window was open, he said.

Dunn immediately objected on the grounds that the witness was not an expert on criminology and that he had a great deal to gain by saying what he said. The judge agreed and sustained the objection. Tell indicated that he had no further questions and went back to where he had been seated.

Dunn, responding to the judge's direction, came up to the witness box. She paused for a moment then asked Iota why he had run after Shaw and why he was in the men's room at the time of Shaw's murder. He responded that it was nature that had been responsible not him; the courtroom erupted in laughter at his response and Ford banged his gavel threatening to clear the audience if there were any further outbursts.

Dunn proceeded. She asked him other questions about the open window, whether there was anybody else in the men's room, and why he just stood there when he could have helped Sparks.

Iota met each one of the assertions by saying that he didn't know. Dunn continued with her questions. Although she was very surprised that Tell had called Iota to the stand she knew that this was her chance of bringing up some issues that had bothered her.

"Are you a homosexual?" The whole courtroom was shocked at this question.

"Are you serious?"

"Yes I am. Are you gay?" She had planned to ask him this question if she ever had the chance.

Tell immediately objected but the judge overruled it. Tell was afraid that this might happen since Ford and Dunn had the relationship that they had.

"I don't know what you're talking about," Iota replied.

"Very well. Did you ever see the earring that the cops took from Shaw's pocket?" Tell smiled at this question. It meant that he would not have any difficulty bringing up the issue of the earring and that Megan Sullivan's suicide could be interpreted as a sign that she was the murderer. The earring was very attractive and it could be worn by a gay person. That was her point. When Tell realized what was going on, he slinked in his chair. He immediately turned to his second, a lawyer by the name of John Leaming, and he said that they had better get in touch with Cappy, Muldoon and Pierce in order to get to the truth. Despite his use of the law for his own ends, Tell was basically an honorable man.

She said that she was finished with Iota and returned to her seat. She was very pleased at her performance. She recalled one day in law school how the professor had told her that if she didn't know where to go, improvise. Always improvise, he said. She sat down with a smile on her face.

Tell's face was ashen at this point. He had wanted to use Sullivan's suicide as something that indicated that maybe she was the responsible person. In this way, he might have influenced Scott, the carpenter whom he already selected as a member of the jury. Could Scott, thinking about Sullivan committing suicide, influence the other members of the jury to vote for acquittal? At the very least, Tell thought, Scott could raise the issue and the resultant doubt in the jury could result in a mistrial. At least Tell was thinking in this direction.

The judge banged his gavel and called it a day when Ann had sat down. She and the rest of the courtroom stood up as the judge left the bench.

CHAPTER TWENTY FIVE

When he left the bench, Ford returned to his office. Ann waited until the entire courtroom was empty. Even Tell had left for the day while Ann sat in the prosecutor's space reading her notes. When the courtroom had emptied out, she got up from her chair and went to the judge's chamber. Instead of knocking on the door as was the customary way that lawyers usually abided by; she burst right in. He was waiting for her. He grabbed her fiercely and began to kiss her passionately on the neck. She objected saying that they should be careful and go to his place which was only a few blocks away.

Meanwhile, Tell had gone to his car and proceeded to go to Judge Ford's condo. Tell parked across the street from his home out of sight. He felt badly about spying the way that he was doing but thought that he might catch them engaging in some fishy behavior. When the car pulled up in the driveway to the condo, Tell noticed that the two of them were seated close to one another. She had her winter jacket on; it gets chilly in the fall in Boston. When they got out of the car, he noticed that Ford had a very stern look on his face, but that was not unusual for someone who wears a judge's robe. But that was not what he was looking for. He wanted some further kind of intimacy, something that he could use at the trial when he called for a mistrial. Everybody knew, he thought, about the relation between Judge Ford and Dunn, at least the lawyers knew about it. He was looking for evidence of wrong doing. All he had to do was to tell the jury about them and there would be a mistrial. The trick was to get people to believe that Ford had acted recklessly in his relation to Ann. That was not an easy task.

He waited as they got out of the car and went inside the condo. He waited for over an hour and then he saw Ann Dunn running down the street and hailing a cab. He thought that this was a strange thing for her to do. She didn't even have her jacket on.

When Ford and Dunn went inside the condo, Ford was acting strangely. He was not like he was. She asked him what was wrong and he answered that his life had very little meaning for him now. He went to his desk and pulled out a gun from one of the drawers. When Dunn saw this she began to panic. She screamed out asking him what he was doing.

She never liked guns and thought that they were a scourge on society. She was adamant about this. Never use a gun was her way of thinking. She thought that organizations like the National Rifle association prolong this scourge and now its philosophy could be used to cut short the life of someone she truly loved. The judge was intent on taking his own life.

She had thought that they would make love when they got to the condo. She was very excited about this and the possible repercussions of making love with him. She was a quite a forward lady and she was more than willing to take the first step. Even if that meant that she would be the one who proposed marriage. She never minded, but here he was holding a gun; the man she loved. A gun! What was he doing with a gun? Wasn't their relationship at all meaningful to him? She stammered and stuttered. She asked him why; what did he want to do holding a gun? What was this all about?

"Why are you doing this?" She screamed at him as he looked blankly around the room. What could he have been thinking? He began to cry. He said something about Kennedy, how he had lost his best friend. He said that he was sick of being a judge finding some people guilty and others not guilty. Dunn responded to this display of self-pity by saying that Kennedy had nothing to do with his own assassination. He couldn't have. She screamed that Ford was a good man and that he was a good and fine judge; a decent man and that without him the court would not be the same. She began to cry as he put the gun to his forehead. She begged him not to do anything so stupid. She pleaded with him. She said that she loved him and if he loved her, he would not do what she feared that he might. He smiled at her, a very weak smile. His eyes were swollen and bloodshot as he pondered what he would do next. He brought the gun slowly to his forehead and pulled the trigger. He was dead before his body hit the floor.

Dunn screamed. She had never thought that their relationship would end this way. She kept saying no, no, no, he could not have done that. She screamed out that he could not have done that. They had been lovers for a long time. Ever since they first were introduced to one another at a party held in the governor's mansion, they felt that they were meant for each other. They would take advantage of the courtroom where they both worked and make love. She would invariably go into his chambers on a ruse, and they would relate sexually to one another. She could not get him out of her head; he could not get her out of his head. All the other lawyers knew what was going on, and they would talk and joke about it when they got together in the lawyers lounge.

One weekend they had gone away to Maine. They got a room at one of the many hotels that were vacant. It was a chilly weekend in October. The motel that they stayed at was called The Drop Anchor and there were not many people there the weekend that they went. They spent the entire time making love and watching television. They had asked for a king sized bed when they got to the Drop Anchor because they both were intent on making love all the time. And that's what they did.

When they registered with the girl at the front desk they both knew that it was too cold to go swimming but they didn't mind. They were alone. And no expectations were forced on them. They could do what they wanted to and making love was a priority for both of them. The girl at the desk, Moira, was uninterested when she asked how they would pay, whether by credit card or cash, and what kind of a bed they wanted, single or king size.

They made love for the entire weekend. When the girl who cleaned their room came in she announced that her name was Siobhan and that she had come from Ireland and that she only wanted to clean up the room. Of course, they stopped their love making and waited for the girl to pick up and do the essentials that cleaning people do.

But now the situation was different. It was not the same as it was in the little motel in Maine. He had pulled the trigger on a gun and had killed himself. She was horrified at this and tears flooded down her cheek. She didn't know what to do. She thought that she should call the police. She went over to the phone and dialed the police department. Hysterically, she said that someone had committed suicide. She gave the address then she went over to Ford's body and, with her tears streaming, said that she loved him. With that, she still didn't know what to do, so she ran out of the condo without bothering to put on her winter jacket. She just wanted to run away from the whole scene. She ran, she ran and ran. It is a strange thing that the person whom she may have loved at one time becomes the reason for her fleeing from him. But all she knew was that she loved him and now he was dead.

When Tell saw her running he thought that he had better go into the condo and see why she was running. He was concerned. He left his car and went into the condo and saw the judge lying dead on the floor. After registering his shock at what he saw, he now understood why Dunn was running without her winter coat. He immediately went to the phone and called the police dialing 911; he knew a woman would answer the phone. He was still shocked as he told her that someone was either murdered or had committed suicide, he didn't want to tell her that it was a judge who was the person involved. She said that the police would be right over after she asked him the address.

They arrived shortly after the call. Detective Robert Marion was accompanied by five other officers. Marion told the man holding the camera to take photos of the body first, then the entire room. He also told him to take a photo of Tell who protested that he was an attorney and that he represented Mark Iota who was on trial. Marion said that he didn't care, that he didn't give a damn, as he directed another policeman to make sure that the physical evidence was intact including the empty shell case that they found on the floor. He also told the man with the camera to make sure that he took a photo of Tell. After Tell had protested that taking his photo would interfere with representing Iota, he told Marion that attorney Dunn had been somehow involved and that he had seen her running down the street without her winter jacket which the police had found on the floor beside the body of Ford.

Marion said that she was a person of interest if they determined that Ford's death was murder. If it was a suicide, Ford's decision would exonerate her and that he could understand her fleeing from the scene. Tell was not sure if Marion knew of the relationship that Ford had with Dunn, but he went along with what he had said and that it didn't make any difference if he knew of the relation or not. The fact was that Ford was dead.

When they had finished their investigation, they called for someone to take the body to the morgue. Tell had assumed that they had called the people at the morgue since they were the ones who were ordinarily charged with that responsibility. When they arrived, they were very efficient in placing the body in a body bag and taking it away with them. Tell remained for Marion's questions. He asked him why he was there and Tell answered that he was investigating why Ford had left the trial of Iota with Dunn. If it had to have something to do with the trial then he had every right to be there. When he saw Dunn running down the street, he knew that something was wrong, so he left his car and went into the condo where he saw Ford's body and that's all he had seen. Marion shrugged his shoulders saying that there was no reason to hold him and so he let him go.

When the judge said that the trial would commence the next day, Tell had accepted that. Now he left the building where the judge's body lies, he got into his car and drove away.

CHAPTER TWENTY SIX

Tell arrived at the courtroom the next day. His thoughts were on Ford and the fact that he took his own life. He said to himself that he could not understand anybody taking his or her own life, let alone the judge of this trial. He was still very bothered by Ford's suicide and had the awful feeling that somehow Ann Dunn had something to do with it.

He had gotten up early, made coffee, and parked his car in front of the courtroom building. When he entered the courtroom, he was surprised that there were so many people there, including reporters. They probably were there because the trial had been such a sensation. Reports of the trial were on television news and in the newspapers. The clerk of the court came into the courtroom. He announced Ford's death at his own hands. He said that another judge would be assigned the case and that everyone would be notified.

Mark Iota was dressed in a shirt and tie as he sat in the accused chair. He was obviously waiting for Tell who eventually took his seat next to him. After they had exchanged pleasantries, Tell asked him why he looked so pale. The answer was obvious. He was still recovering from the party that his father had thrown for him.

Reporters literally had begged their bosses for the opportunity to attend the party that Mr. Iota had thrown for his son, rather than going to the trial which was scheduled in the daytime rather than at night. Parties occur in the evening and generally there is liquor and food. The party was held at Iota's residence and Mr. Iota was the host.

The party was attended by people other than reporters though. The girls were all there including Gabriella, Haley and Samantha. The guys who were friendly with Iota were all there; Bill Galvin, Barry Sparks, and Steve Long. Even Arthur Pierce came to the party. Mr. Iota thought that it would be a good idea to have a party for his son. Tell had told Mr. Iota that he couldn't come to the party. He told Mr. Iota that Ford had committed suicide. Tell said that he wanted to get some rest. He was very tired. And he was very busy, he said. Otherwise he would be happy to attend; of course he was just being polite. The suicide of Ford bothered Tell immensely. Ford's suicide immediately became the topic of the conversation at the party. But, as with any bad news, pretty soon it seems to go away and disappear. People at a party eventually begin to dance and sing no matter what the reason for the party is.

Mr. Iota had said that the party was for his son who was innocent of the crime of murder. He said that he may be gay but he did not kill Shaw. He said this as he poured everybody a fresh drink and put music on the phonograph.

"Come on everybody. This is a party. I have gone to great lengths arranging it," he said to all the partygoers.

Gradually, they all began to feel more at ease and began to enjoy the music, drink and talk about things other than Ford's suicide. Even Pierce began to dance with the girls. Maybe it was the alcohol that was more the reason for his asking Gabriella to dance than his own choice, but soon he was dancing with her and he had asked the other girls if they wanted to dance as well. Pretty soon he and everybody else were dancing and singing songs especially the song which praised Savan College, "We will fight for old Savan till they all come home."

When Gabriella was through dancing with Pierce, she went into the kitchen. She put on a pot of coffee even though it was not her home. The coffee began to boil so she put the stove off. She poured herself a cup and savored the taste that freshly brewed coffee often brings. As she was sipping the coffee she thought of a number of questions that she ought to ask Mark Iota. She was not aware that he was the murderer of Shaw. She went into the dining room where the dancing had stopped and asked Iota if he would come into the kitchen.

When he came into the kitchen, she poured him a cup of coffee and said that she didn't know if he wanted something else to go with it.

"Do you want anything else? It's your kitchen after all," she said.

"No, I'm fine. The coffee is enough," he replied.

"I called you in here because I want to ask you a question. I hope you don't mind."

"No I don't," he answered.

"Tell me, remember the night that we met? I was dating Barry Sparks at the time. I don't date him anymore. But I was wondering why you had asked about the murder of Shaw and the earring in his pocket. Also, why did you ask about Megan's suicide and the open window in the men's room?"

"I don't know. I was just curious."

"Oh ok, nothing else then. I was just interested in why you had asked those questions, is all."

Iota felt at ease with Gabriella. Perhaps it was because she had brought up Shaw's murder. He went on to talk more about it and told

Gabriella that he was sorry that he went into the men's room at that time. He said that if he had waited until Shaw had left the men's room, Shaw would still be alive. Iota had been drinking heavily and was quite willing to say anything to her. He said that Shaw had been his boyfriend and he began to tease him by showing him the earring that Shaw had taken from his date's room and teasing him about it. He said that he couldn't stand it any longer and that he took out the gun from his pocket that he took from his father's display case in order to show the guys and be more popular with them and shot Shaw with it. He told Gabriella that he was sorry for what he had done.

Gabriella screamed! She didn't want to hear what he had just told her. The rest of the party rushed into the kitchen in response to her repeated screams. They were shocked when Gabriella told them what Iota had said and that he admitted to killing Shaw. She was in a state of shock at what Iota had told her. The state of shock would last for a very long time. Nobody could believe it. They kept saying that that information must be a joke of sorts but the wrong kind of humor. It must be an attempt by Iota to meet with Ford's suicide. But it was not funny. And they told him so.

He said that it wasn't a joke. He had killed Shaw because Shaw was his boyfriend and had cheated on him with a girl. He had even showed Iota the girl's earring and teased him about it. Besides, legally it doesn't matter. Shaw is still dead and with Ford committing suicide the case would be called a mistrial and would not affect him. He was safe, he said, and people should not worry about him. The people at the party told him that they were more concerned about Shaw and his family than they were about him and that according to the law if a person admits to any crime to more than one person other than his lawyer, then any deal or any talk about a mistrial was obviated and the accused could still go to trial if the prosecutor wants him to. They all looked at Iota with heavy disdain when they told him this, all but Mr. Iota who was in a state of shock.

Mr. Iota had rushed into the kitchen along with the other people when they heard Gabriella scream. But he was not prepared for what Mark had told the people. His own and his only son was the accused murderer of Shaw at Savan. He still had difficulty believing it. When he first learned of Ford's suicide he was tempted to call off the party, and now he thought that it would have been the best thing for him to do. He had no idea that the party would end this way with his son admitting to Shaw's murder and that both of them were gay lovers. It didn't bother him but he thought that it would be best for everybody to leave.

They all left abruptly. Gabriella and the girls left without saying anything to one another. They all expressed their concerns about Mark Iota's confession of the crime of murder to Gabriella when he admitted to the crime in the kitchen of his own home. That bothered them, that he would admit something so horrendous in his own kitchen.

The next day the courtroom was abuzz with the news of Ford's suicide. The chatter was all about Ford's suicide. Tell sat beside Iota on the defendant's side. Brian Murphy was the new prosecutor and he sat on the other side. He was a graduate of Providence College and went to law school at the Catholic University of America in Washington, D. C. before he was hired as a prosecutor by the Attorney General of Massachusetts.

CHAPTER TWENTY SEVEN

As he had promised, the clerk of the court notified all of the people when the unfinished trial would be held. The newspapers did the same. The spaces in practically all the papers were consumed with news of the trial.

Tell arrived in the courtroom and took a seat beside Mark Iota. He looked directly at him. He expressed his horror at Iota's confession to Gabriella. He told him that when a defendant tells another person other than his lawyer, it does away with any prior decision that the court may have made. Whether or not a mistrial occurs is up to the judge and the prosecutor, but it was foolish to confess to Gabriella, he said. Anything at all could result in a mistrial; it is especially stupid when the accused admits to the killing that he or she has been accused of. What kind of a fool would do that, he asked. Iota sat quietly. He didn't respond to Tell's criticism. Tell was visibly angry with Iota. He said that with Ford's suicide, he was depressed and that the judge who would take Ford's place could announce a mistrial and the prosecutor could make a decision to retry the case. A re-trial was assured now that Iota had made his confession to Gabriella.

And there would be another prosecutor because Ann Dunn had some kind of relationship with Ford. He looked over at Murphy when he said that. Murphy didn't respond instead he kept his gaze in front of him. Tell then looked around the courtroom while the jury filed in and took their seats in the jury box.

Then the judge came into the courtroom after being announced by the clerk and after everybody had stood up as was the customary thing to do. Tell wondered who would take Ford's place. The judge ambled over to his bench as he told the people in the courtroom to be seated. To Tell's surprise it was Judge Carl Oblanski who took Ford's place, who was, in the opinion of most of the lawyers, very rigid and conservative in his rulings. Tell had the same opinion.

The judge immediately said that with Ford's death, he had been assigned the case and there was some concern about the relationship between Ford and Dunn. Whether there would be a mistrial depended on a number of things he said from the bench; the relationship between

Ford and the prosecutor Ann Dunn, whether the accused had admitted to the crime, whether he had told someone other than his lawyer, and finally, whether a member of the jury had in any way compromised his or her pledge to remain open-minded in considering the evidence given at the trial. It's up to the prosecutor if he or she wants to pursue the trial further, he proclaimed. He said that he was declaring a mistrial because of the relationship between Ford and Dunn and that the trial of the accused would be held as soon as a new jury could be chosen, if the prosecutor agreed. The witnesses would all have to be recalled he said.

Tell was delighted with this decision. It would mean that not only did he have the opportunity to review his opening remarks to the jury but also that he would have the chance to review all of the witnesses of the trial. He still felt that his client, Mark Iota, would be found not guilty of the crime despite his confession to Gabriella when he made it to her in his very own kitchen

The prosecutor had called for a new jury. When the new date had been selected, there was a great deal of excitement in the air. Reporters from all over the country were scurrying to gain entrance into the courtroom. Apparently, the trial had gained national attention. Many were denied access to the courtroom despite their pleas. There simply was not enough room.

Shaw's family was there; his mother, father and several cousins. They all glared at Iota and at Tell. When they were asked by a reporter what they thought of the trial and Ford's suicide, the mother of Shaw broke down in tears.

Tell took his seat beside the defendant and called the first witness, Clyde Longquist, also known as Cappy. After taking the oath that he would testify to only what he considered was true, he took his seat in the witness box. Tell then began his questions.

"Your name is Clyde Longquist but people call you Cappy, is that correct?"

"Yes sir, it is."

"Did you find anything strange about the murder that you investigated?"

"Yes sir, I did."

"Would you tell the jury what that was?"

"Yes sir, I will. I began by going to the scene of the crime and found the accused standing beside the body. The window was open and I directed one of the officers to conduct an investigation of the grounds outside."

"Did the officer find anything?"

"Yes he did."

"Would you tell the jury what he found?"

"Yes. It was a gun."

"So, he found a gun outside. What did you do next?'

"I took the gun and made sure that it was sent to the evidence office to make a determination if the gun was the one used in the shooting. I also fished into the pocket of the deceased. I found an earring, only one."

"Ah hah! So is it possible that the earring had something to do with the shooting?"

"Yes sir, I became obsessed with the earring."

"You became obsessed. And did that lead to anything?"

"Yes it did. Further examination of it, the earring I mean, led me and others to investigate who it belonged to and why it was in Shaw's pocket."

"And what did you conclude?"

Murphy objected to this line of questioning particularly after the last question on grounds that it required a conclusion. The judge agreed and sustained the objection. And so it went. Tell would ask a question, Murphy would object on some ground and the judge would agree with him. Tell's response was simply to smile at the judge's decision. Tell felt that the more Murphy objected, and the more that the judge sustained the objection and, in effect, overruled what Tell or the witness had said, the more the jury would be on his side. People tend to root for the underdog.

Tell then asked Cappy what he had concluded about the earring. Cappy, admitting to his obsession with the earring, commented that the girl who had committed suicide was sure that the earring in a box in her room was a match to the one that he had fished out of Shaw's pocket. When he was asked by Tell whether it was possible that the owner of the earring could have hidden somewhere, for example in a stall in the men's room, until Shaw came into the men's room and then shot him before throwing the gun out the window, Cappy said that anything was possible. Tell, smiling at his response, expecting an objection from Murphy which didn't come, commented that after all Iota was not the only one charged with the crime that the dean of discipline of Savan had undergone the rigors of a trial as well and was found innocent. Cappy answered by simply saying that he agreed. Murphy objected furiously to the use of a prior trial in questioning the witness and to the witness's response. He, in effect, demanded that judge Oblanski intervene in the questioning, but the judge did not.

Murphy got up from his chair and faced Cappy when the judge offered him the opportunity. The judge was very meticulous when it came to courtroom procedures; when the defense is finished with a witness the other side is offered the chance to ask him questions. Murphy began his questioning of Cappy by asking him what his role was in the investigation, why he was involved. Cappy answered that he had gone to the men's room at Savan and found Shaw dead from a gunshot wound with Iota standing next to his body, and that the window of the restroom was open. Murphy next asked him if he had made any arrests and Cappy said that he didn't. Murphy asked him why he made no arrests and Cappy responded by saying that he had no reason to. Murphy said that it was unusual for a police detective not to make an arrest and Cappy agreed. At which point he shrugged and he said that he had no further questions for Cappy.

Cappy then left the witness box.

After Cappy had given his testimony, Tell called Muldoon to the stand to testify that what Cappy had said was consistent with the notes that Muldoon had taken in reference to the other witnesses that Tell had called. They were the boys who were in some way involved with the crime, Bill Galvin, Barry Sparks and Steve Long. Tell had also called Gabriella, and the other girls. He was obviously thinking that the more witnesses that he called to the witness box, the better were the chances that he would win.

When Gabriella was sworn in by the clerk, Tell asked her if she had gone to the party that Mr. Iota had thrown for his son. She answered that she had and then Tell asked her what happened at the party. She said that she had called Mark into the kitchen on another matter and that Mark had confessed to killing Shaw. When the other party goers heard about this and when, especially, Mr. Iota was informed, they were all upset. They were very upset, she said. Those who were there by invitation left the party. Mr. Iota, obviously, didn't leave his own house, Gabriella said. He had expected Gabriella to say that they all had a good time celebrating the fact that Mark was to be found not guilty and that the trial would be called a mistrial.

And so this trial proceeded with Tell and Murphy at odds with one another. Sometimes Murphy would shout at Tell, and there were times Tell would give him an innocent look. Murphy would demand that the judge rule on an objection that had been made. Tell just smiled at these moments; he had hoped that the jury would see him as a mild and considerate man rather than a pugnacious sort who was upset when things did not go his way.

The trial lasted for three days after Pierce had testified along with the boys and girls whom Tell had called to the witness box to testify to

Mark's character. Finally, the judge had given his instructions to the jury and told them to go to the room which had been set aside for them, and to be certain about their verdict. He told members of the jury that they should be proud of their service to the State in light of how difficult their service was.

Murphy and Tell, along with the other lawyers who had participated in the trial, waited in the lawyer's room for the verdict. Tell thought of what one of his professors told him about truth that no matter how difficult it is, it is always better to speak the truth than to use lies in what you do. Tell simply smiled.

The jury was deliberating on the first day, the second day and on the third day. Tell had been in the lawyer's room during the daytime, but at night, when the jury had all gone home, he sat at the bar at the Guild and Feather, sipping a vodka and tonic. One night the girl, Deirdre, came into the bar and pulled up a stool and sat beside him. She began the conversation by saying that he looked familiar. He told her that they had spoken before. He was still rather embarrassed because she looked so young; she was at an age where going to a bar was the thing to do and she went to the Guild and Feather almost every night. Perhaps it was to meet a man, Tell thought. But he recognized the difference in age when he left her sitting there and he left the bar.

He wondered when the jury would return its verdict. They had been deliberating for a long time now. He further thought that the longer they deliberated, the better chance he would have of them finding his client not guilty. At least, he continued to think, they might be deadlocked with his carpenter friend voting for acquittal while the rest of the jury had voted that his client was guilty. He didn't know. It is always a guess when you try to figure out what another person or people are thinking. He buckled up his seat belt and drove to his condo. He drove there quickly, more quickly than he usually did, and got out of his car when he arrived, still thinking about the verdict of the jury. Was the time that they were taking an indication of their deadlock, or were they stuck on a testimony of one of the witnesses? He didn't know. At this point he didn't care much as he got ready for bed. He knew that he would sleep well.

The next day he was awakened by the phone. The person on the other end said that the jury had reached its verdict and would bring it to the judge when he came into the courtroom, which would be about 1:00 o'clock in the afternoon. Tell quickly got dressed, had a cup of coffee, and headed for the courthouse. He was anxious now. When he arrived at his destination, he immediately went to the lawyer's room. It seemed to him that he had spent his entire life there. When the jury came in, Tell and the other lawyers who were assembled there were informed. They began their march into the courtroom.

The judge came into the courtroom with a docile look on his face. He was ready to accept the verdict of the jury, whatever it was, and get on with things. He was tired of the trial, and it showed. The jury came in and took their seats. The judge asked the jury foreman if the jury had reached a verdict. When he was informed that they had, he had the clerk of courts bring the paper with the verdict on it to him. The jury foreman, or should I say forewoman, was a 42 year old widow who relished her time on the jury.

He looked at the paper and the docile look on his face disappeared. He told the clerk to bring the paper back to the chairperson of the jury and asked her the question that many accused feared. After he told the accused and the accused lawyers to stand, he asked the chairperson to read the verdict.

Nervously she read the verdict.

"In the matter of the murder charge against the defendant, Mark Iota, we the jury as established according to Massachusetts's law, finds the defendant guilty as charged."

Tell was astonished at this decision. He was livid. He was angry at his own preparation and the decision of the jury. He thought that he could have done a better job in defending his client and that the jury would have returned with another decision of not guilty. He and the other lawyers, who were a part of the defense team, could not believe what the chair person had read. When the judge asked whether everyone on the jury agreed and they all nodded their assent, he immediately sentenced Mark Iota to life in the prison at Walpole without a chance of the possibility of parole. He said that there was no point in waiting another few weeks to hand out the sentence.

Tell balked at this decision as well as the chairperson's statement which had announced guilt. He had assumed that his carpenter friend would, at the least, cause a mistrial. Tell was convinced that his carpenter friend would vote to find Mark not guilty and thus cause a mistrial in the event that the other members of the jury voted to find him guilty. He was certain of this. But the jury had spoken its decision and had found the defendant guilty as charged.

Mark's father was equally shocked at the verdict. He thought for sure that the jury would find him innocent of the crime. In his mind, he thought that Tell had done a masterful job at his son's defense and that the jury would find him innocent. He was convinced of this, but he was incorrect.

Mark Iota smiled at the verdict and appeared to be pleased with it. Murphy accepted the congratulations of the other lawyers who had been working with him. After he had accepted their warm congratulations, he left the courtroom. One never knows if people are sincere in their praise or if they are being insincere. Mark had the same look on his face as he had the night he met Barry and Gabriella. To Gabriella, this was scary. She felt that he was a strange person and could do very strange things, even in prison. Mark was led out of the courtroom by guards. He had handcuffs on and was shackled by his feet and it made walking very difficult. But he managed to go with the guard to the waiting bus downstairs from the courtroom. The bus had been waiting for the verdict by the jury in Mark's case and it contained others, who were criminals now, who had been found guilty of various crimes. These criminals were found guilty of crimes ranging from murder to stealing property. Their trials took place in the same courthouse that had found Mark Iota guilty of the crime of murder.

Mark got on the bus and appeared very calm; in fact he began to sing.

Chapter Twenty Eight

He sang the song "John Brown's Body". The text included the words, "His truth goes marching on." Iota apparently thought that the killing of Robert Shaw was ok when he sang. He laughed out loud and kept on singing, much to the irritability of the others on the bus who told him to shut up. But he kept it up singing the words to the song,

"Glory, glory, halleluiah, his truth goes marching on."

The others on the bus became increasingly more and more angry at Iota and his singing, despite the fact that they were all handcuffed they began to brawl. The guards reacted quickly as they attempted to break up the fight. The fight involved, not only Iota and the other people on the bus but it also involved a man by the name of Steve Brown. Brown was convicted of money fraud on one of his former employers in a separate trial than that of Iota. He was sentenced to five years in the prison at Walpole. One could tell that he was fed up with Iota's singing, particularly the song that he was singing.

Brown was a big, black man who was riled whenever he heard anyone singing, especially when they sang anything about John Brown or anyone who had anything to do with the civil rights movement. He was even opposed to Martin Luther King and his rhetoric. He was six foot, four and weighed two hundred and forty pounds. He was not someone whom you would want to upset.

Peace was finally restored on the bus. It proceeded to go to the prison at Walpole which was only eight miles from the courthouse. When it got there, there were a slew of armed guards waiting for it. They were assembled there in order to prevent any violence or an attempted escape by any of the convicts. Convicts . . . . this was a term that would be used for the passengers on the bus from this moment on . . . . and it was a term that would be used to describe Iota for the rest of his life.

The first thing that Mark had to do was to shower and get detoxified with the hose that they had at the prison for that purpose. He relished the shower, but took exception to the process of detoxification. He didn't like being hosed down. The pressure of the hose that was used was like being watered down by the entire fire department. He didn't like it at all. After he had taken a shower and had undergone the process of detoxification, he was given the clothing that he would wear now as a prisoner. After he dressed and he was summoned to the warden's office. The warden wanted to see him.

The warden was an average sized man. He was well dressed in a shirt and tie and his shoes were brightly shined. It was certainly a contrast to Iota. When Iota came into his office the warden laid down the rules for him in detail and told him that he was expected to follow them completely. The rules included the expectation that all prisoners would be expected to refrain from any singing or any expressions of discontent with the prison's policies. He gave him a number of rules. They also detailed how prisoners should respond to visitors when they came and the process that visitors should follow. The warden stood in sharp contrast to Iota. He was well dressed; Iota had on his prison uniform.

The warden insisted that when a guest came to visit a prisoner what the proper etiquette was. Prisoners were not to be rude nor should the prisoner be boastful about what he had done or what was going on at the prison. Prisoners were not allowed to tell anyone what they did in prison at Walpole. Nobody was excused from these rules. If somebody came to visit the prison, the prisoner was to be polite and respectful. When a visitor came, or when groups of visitors came to see a convict, the visitor or the groups of visitors were herded in a common room before they saw anybody whom he or they had come to visit. The doors closed in both the front section and in the rear section before they were allowed in the visitor's area. Visitors were not allowed to wander in the prison unattended.

The warden asked Iota if he understood these rules. Iota said that he did and the warden dismissed him from his office. He slowly got up from his chair and he left the room. He was escorted by a guard through the ground floor of the prison. It had prison cells throughout the area. The cells all looked ominous to Iota. He glanced up to where they shot up from the first floor where he was walking. There were three tiers of cells. Iota was assigned to a cell on the first tier on the ground floor. When he got to the cell that would be his home for the rest of his life, he stood outside and gasped. He stood shocked at what he was seeing. The guard who was his escort began to scold him firmly for this behavior. Iota remained standing and gasping. He appeared to be stunned. His cellmate was Steve Brown! Brown stood in the opened cell laughing. His shadow was almost as big as he was.

Brown welcomed Iota to the cell. He said that he should enjoy the palatial pleasures and the wonderful environment that the cell offered. Of course he was being sarcastic. He said that this was Iota's home.

He didn't realize that this was to be Iota's home for the rest of his life. Brown had only five years to be Iota's cellmate. He was also not aware that Iota, his intended cellmate, was homosexual. The guard said that his responsibilities were over now that Iota had a cellmate, and left. Iota remained standing outside of the cell and he appeared to be in a trance. Brown told him to enter the cell and they could begin their relationship.

The cell was about ten by ten feet. In that small space it had a desk to write on, a sink and a toilet. There were several electrical outlets in the cell. These outlets could be used to plug in a light or whatever else the convict had in mind. He could use these outlets to plug in an electric clock or a television set. Brown had a television set.

Iota looked outside the cell. He wanted to see what he would be facing for the rest of his life. He looked out above him and saw the almost endless tiers that were there. They were dirty and gloomy. Outside here were weights for the prisoners to use and a homemade basketball court with a backboard and a homemade net. That was it. The area gave one the impression of what the dust bowl of the early thirties in the mid-western states was like.

Surrounding the area were several towers where guards with rifles were situated. They had rifles in order to shoot at prisoners who tried to escape or who did not follow the rules of prison behavior that were set down by the warden. Only one prisoner tried to escape during his tenure by digging his way out through a tunnel. The convicts considered the rules that he had established as discriminatory. And they all thought that he should be a convict like them. In that way, they thought, he would see that his rules were not fair.

Brown was much bigger and stronger than Iota. He demonstrated his superior strength by telling him to take the upper bunk. Iota obliged and he put his two towels, facecloth and change of underwear on the bunk. He said that he was sorry for any commotion that his singing caused on the bus, that he didn't mean any harm to anyone. He said that as Brown continued to glare at him.

Brown finally told Iota not to take the top bunk. Instead, he should sleep with him in the lower bunk. Brown was not gay, but that was a common practice in the prison. Brown learned that very quickly. Men related to men as husbands related to their wives. In the prison at Walpole this was the ordinary form of behavior.

Iota was pleased with this arrangement.

CHAPTER TWENTY NINE

Days faded into days as Iota was becoming accustomed to prison life. He worked in the library staking books. He slept with Brown at night taking care of his homosexual needs and Brown's heterosexual ones. They related to one another even though one was homosexual and the other was heterosexual. Brown was the aggressor. Iota enjoyed this. He had a number of homosexual experiences in the showers. As a matter of fact, he looked forward to these experiences as well.

Life had never been as good for him as it was in prison. He was convinced of this. He worked in the library which had a number of books that he had wanted to read, and he took them out of the library and read them at night before he went to bed with Brown relating to him sexually. Brown spent most nights watching television before he related to Iota. He had brought the television set with him. The prison code not only allowed television but also encouraged its use. The prison however only allowed television sets that were less than 14 inches. It did this, while encouraging its use, in order to prevent riots in the prison. It seemed to work. The last prison riot was ten years ago.

There were also things to do outside. Convicts had constructed a crude basketball net, backboard and semi-court. Of course, the guards, from the watchtowers with their rifles, were ready to fire them and break up any fights that may occur between the prisoners. These guards were supported by the regular guards from inside the prison walls which was unusual since being a watch guard was looked upon as good duty.

One day Iota sat on top of a picnic bench that was available for the convicts to use as they choose. It was rundown and the dirty ground where it stood had wood chips all over it. But Iota didn't mind. It gave him a nice view of the basketball game that Brown played in. Brown played well. He was big and strong and he had a good outside shot. Generally, when he shot the ball, it went in the basket. But, of course, he missed from time to time. He drove to the basket well as Iota cheered. On one play, Brown was driving toward the basket when one of the other players foolishly attempted to impede his path. Brown ran right over him. They got into a fist fight and Brown knocked him out. The guards from the watchtowers did little to quell the fight, but the regular guards from inside the prison walls intervened and beat Brown and the other fellow with their clubs. They beat both so badly that they had to be taken to the prison hospital for treatment. They both received stiches to their wounds. Most of these wounds were from the beatings that the guards had inflicted upon them. Iota remained sitting where he was. He didn't stand up, he didn't even want to. He just sat there. He was unmoved by the beating that Brown had taken.

There also was a chapel where one could pray, and a meeting room where AA and NA meetings were held. This room was a very popular room with the inmates and they used it often. It was just below the cell where Brown and Iota's cell was.

On one rainy day, Brown decided that he would go to the meeting room to see what was happening there. He left the cell and walked to the room. He walked down the flight of stairs and he looked around. Then he casually went into the room. He didn't go as a drug addict or alcoholic, rather he went out of curiosity. He wanted to see what happened there.

When he came into the room, members of various groups were there already. There were assorted drug addicts who were intent on giving up their habit and a gaggle of recovering alcoholics. The room was arranged with chairs that were placed in a semicircle. To Brown's chagrin, the person who acted as chairperson of the meeting was the same guy whom he got into a fight with on the basketball court. The chairperson opened the meeting by asking everybody there to join him in saying the Serenity Prayer. It goes:

"God grant me the Serenity to accept things I cannot change
Courage to change the things that I can
And wisdom to know the difference."

The chairperson then asked if anyone had anything that they wanted to share. A recovering alcoholic stood up and volunteered to share with the others something about his alcoholism. He began to speak slowly. His story included the expectations that are found in any story that is told at any AA meeting that might have been held outside of the prison walls. According to these standards, a speaker is expected to say that he is an alcoholic and that he had hurt a number of people with his drinking. He spoke generally about his problems with alcohol from the beginning of his addiction until the time that he admitted that he was powerless over alcohol and that he needed God in his life. He included in his talk, the many times when he tried to beat his addiction on his own.

He spoke about the experiences that he had, when he lived by himself over a garage in a small room which had a bed and a piano in it, when he would go through "horrors" by himself. The "horrors", as the term relates to people in AA, includes the physical pain that the alcoholic goes through when he tries to beat the addiction on his own. This would involve day one when the pain is so severe that the alcoholic goes through that he prefers death to this ordeal. The speaker mentioned that he would often, on the first day, look for a weapon to end his life and his suffering.

But he didn't find one and on the second day of these "horrors", he would find the physical effects on his body. This would be later classified by a psychiatrist, whom the speaker saw after he had experienced these "horrors", as convulsions that showed that the body needed alcohol. In its absence, it would reveal itself in black and blue marks all over the body. The speaker also talked about these.

He also spoke about the time when he had attended a conference for alcoholics that was held in one of the motels in upper state New York. During this period of time, he was the only person among the alcoholics who had assembled there who was drinking alcohol. He had gone to a seminar for people interested in buying one of the units of the motel as a condo. He pretended interest in buying one of the units but he was not so much as interested in buying a unit as he was in the wine that was being served for anybody that showed an interest in buying one of them.

The speaker also spoke about when he tried to get people down to the pool at the same meeting. He had been drinking all day and had shouted up to the other nondrinking alcoholics to come down to the pool. He had a drink in his hand. He kept on shouting for them to come down and join him. They were assembled on the balcony above the swimming pool and were on a break from their meetings. They all shook their heads at him in astonishment when he shouted up from the pool for them to come down.

The speaker finished his story, and those who had assembled for the meeting applauded him before they joined hands and said the Our Father. This occurs in any AA meeting on the "outside" where people can come and go as they like.

Brown was depressed when he left the meeting. He felt like a little boy when he does something wrong. He was depressed because he had gone through the same experience himself, although it was not alcohol that caused him the same grief that the speaker had alluded to, but rather drug withdrawal. He still felt depressed; very depressed. He had many thoughts. He thought about the numerous times he took drugs of one type or another and his reaction to them. He felt ashamed. He had read a book a number of years ago that detailed alcohol and drug withdrawal, He was surprised to read that withdrawal from alcohol was more deadly than drug withdrawal. He thought about this often but never more seriously than when the speaker had talked about his withdrawal from alcohol. He hung his head low as he left the meeting and walked to his cell.

There were other purposes for the meeting room. One of the purposes was to show movies. On another night, Brown had expressed interest in seeing a movie, any movie, and had asked Iota to go with him. Iota declined, saying that he had seen the movie that was playing that night a few times and thought that Brown would enjoy it. He said that he had enjoyed the film very much and it still caused shivers to go up and down his spine when he saw it, especially the ending of the film. Film makers are aware that audiences are more interested in how a film ends than they are about any other aspects of a film. He also said that right now he preferred to read the book that he was intent on finishing before he did anything else. Brown shrugged his shoulders and went to the movie by himself.

The film was a murder mystery. It took place in the White House. In fact, the White House was the center of the crime. It took place during the fictional presidency of Oliver Stone.

Apparently Stone, in order to remain the President of the United States of America, had taken the life of his Vice President, William J. Trance. He committed the crime poisoning him during the lunch that they shared daily. When Trance was not looking, the President had suggested that the Vice President examine what was happening on the front lawn, he put poison in his coffee. When the police were called and investigated the murder, they couldn't believe that the President of The United States could possibly be responsible for the murder. So, they charged the waiter who had served the meal with the crime.

The rest of the movie took place in the courtroom. Finally, the President and his role in the crime was discovered.

Chapter Thirty

Brown continued to sit in his chair as the rest of the convicts left the showing, many of them uttering words of distain for the film. They apparently didn't like it at all. Brown continued to sit until the guard told him to get back to his cell.

He thought about his own childhood up to the time that he was a prisoner at Walpole. He was brought up by his mother; his father had left home when he was born never to come back again. He had an older brother. He didn't get along well with him.

When he was a young boy, he was very angry and demonstrated this anger with his aberrant behavior. Even though he had engaged in this kind of behavior, he later went on to Harvard Graduate School after finishing his Boston College degree.

Brown let Iota know how he felt about his childhood when they first met in prison. He told him everything that his father did. He and his brother used to meet his father when he was not drinking. They met him on the front steps of the building where his family lived. His family was not the traditional family. Brown's family consisted of his grandmother, grandfather, two uncles, an aunt, his mother, his brother and two cousins. One night Brown found his father lying unconscious on the front steps of his home and his mother told him to call the police. After he had made the phone call to the Charlestown station, the cops didn't take long coming to his house. His mother had gone inside the house and was sitting on her chair in the living room. The police asked Brown what he wanted to do with his father. He said that his mother didn't want Brown's father and he was not able to take care of him, so the cops shrugged and said that they would take him and they whisked him in the squad car and drove away.

When they got to the station, Brown's father remained unconscious. The policemen thought that he was dead. So they called his brother, who was a state representative, to come to the station to identify him and claim the body. He came immediately. When he got there, Brown's father opened his eyes and asked what the hell he was doing there. This became a part of the Brown's family history. Brown told the story often.

He told Iota the story and Iota laughed much to the chagrin of Brown who looked at family history as something sacred. He had a number of other stories including the time when he and Tony Bartello went to downtown Boston to see a movie after they met with two other guys who were interested in seeing the same film. They got into a fist fight with the two boys because of different versions of the movie. After they had finished with the guys, they left them and came back to Brown's home. Brown's mother asked the boys if they had done anything interesting that night and both boys said that the night was uneventful.

There were many stories that Brown had and many times he was tempted to tell Iota most of them, but time would not allow it. Even though he was sentenced for five years at Walpole, with Iota working in the library and his interest in books generally, he couldn't find the time to tell Iota all the stories even though he felt strongly that stories could be looked at as composing what family life was like for him.

One day, for example, he told Iota the story when he was looking for something to drink. He was a light sleeper and one night, or morning since it was around 3:30am, he found a bottle that his mother had been saving for something special. He took two drinks from it and put water in its place. The next night Reverend Bourque came for a visit and Mrs. Bourque poured him a drink from the bottle. Needless to say what the response was.

Brown had many stories like that and he told them with relish.

CHAPTER THIRTY ONE

One day, as the men were showering, the men began to harass Iota calling him a "fag" and they began to attempt to relate to him sexually both orally and anally. Brown, who had already showered, returned to the shower area and in a booming voice told them in no uncertain terms to stop what they were planning on doing with Iota.

"Stop it! Stop whatever you're thinking! Don't any of you do what you're thinking! He belongs to me!"

The prisoners who had intentions to sexually molest Iota stopped thinking the thoughts that they had as Brown had told them to. He spoke in such a booming voice that anyone would have obeyed. They all feared him with his giant size and they did what he had wanted them to do. They all felt that they would be better off looking for some other victim. Excepting for Iota, the prisoners all left the shower area and proceeded to do what they wanted to do anyhow, but with other victims. From that point on, nobody attempted to do anything to Iota. Nor did they think about it or have any interest in him. Instead, they focused on the young, new prisoners to take care of their "needs". Apart from their sexual interests, they simply went about their own business taking showers and making sure that they were clean.

Iota, when he was at Savan was looked upon as being odd. Despite this he still was accepted by a lot of the students, especially Billy Galvin and Barry Sparks. In prison though, he had assumed a status that he had never known before. And where he was still looked as odd his homosexuality was accepted by many, especially those who were defined, or defined themselves, as homosexual. Convicts couldn't care less if someone was straight or if someone was gay. They only had one thing in mind. They wanted to experience sexual gratification by any means that they could find or with anyone gay or straight. Iota had taken the change in his status gleefully. To him, life was good, even though he had lost his freedom. It was still better than a lot of people had it. It was better than having no job, kids and a wife to support even though he worked in a library stacking books and many people were out of work. They had no job and there was massive unemployment, and had no medical attention. In prison he never worried about wife and kids; he was gay after all. And there was no problem with medical care. In prison one never worried about medical care. There was a hospital and interns available any time, day or night.

After five years had passed, it was time for Brown to be released. He attempted to say goodbye to as many people as he could. He was concerned, especially about Iota. He embraced Iota and told him that it was he who made life in prison bearable. Iota, who thought that life in prison was not that bad, gave him a gentle kiss on the check and he then responded to Brown's hug by tightening his own body. He bid him farewell and said that he would certainly miss him. As Brown left the cell, there were visible tears in Iota's eyes.

Brown proceeded to walk slowly down the hall to the stairs that led out of the prison. On the way, he said goodbye to everyone that he met. He was especially close to another prisoner, who had a cell next to Brown and Iota, and made sure that he said goodbye to him. The cell doors were open, as was the custom whenever someone was released from confinement. Brown entered his friend's cell and embraced him and said his goodbyes. He was very close to him. They shared the same religion and they both suffered from addiction. Both were drug addicts although Brown was sure that he had kicked his habit. His friend was not.

They took turns looking out for Iota. One day, after no one saw Iota for several hours, Brown's friend went to the library looking for him. He found Iota snuggled up with Dante's Inferno. Iota said to Brown's friend that he was intent on finishing the book and lost track of time. Brown's friend took him back to his cell.

Brown told him to take care of himself and to take care of Iota. Then he turned around and left his friend standing in the cell.

Brown went next to the warden's office. The warden, who was new, had left word with the guards that he wanted to see Brown before he left. Ordinarily a prisoner, when he was released, had to go to the Office of the Registrar for the necessary paper work, but this time the warden had intervened. He was concerned about the closeness of Brown and Iota. Brown was big and strong while Iota was smart. Together, they could plan and execute an escape. The warden was very concerned about that as a possibility. Previously, he had two prisoners who had bunked together as Brown and Iota did, one also was big and strong and the other was an extremely intelligent person. They both had escaped and the warden was concerned about the possibility that Iota and Brown would do the same thing. Iota, the warden felt, wanted to have the same relationship with Brown that they had in prison when he was released. Iota wanted to continue to be the intelligent person who could instruct Brown about possible crimes that he could commit on the outside now that he was free to do as he wanted. But Brown had no intention of doing what Iota had wanted him to. As far as he was concerned, the straight and narrow was the only way to go. The warden had all of the necessary papers for Brown to sign. When Brown came into his office and sat down, the warden said that he would escort him to the gates of the prison after he had signed all of the papers that were necessary before he could be released. Brown complied. He took the pen that the warden offered him and signed the necessary papers. At that very moment he considered himself a free man. Afterwards the warden did escort Brown through the prison grounds. The guards in the watchtowers did not aim their rifles since they observed the warden walking with him. They had been informed previously that this was what the warden had wanted. When they got to the main door and it was buzzed open, Brown truly felt free now. But he was worried that he might have become institutionalized in the five years that he spent behind bars.

His former girlfriend was in her car waiting for him. The motor was still running when they embraced. He told her about his confinement and all about Iota. He said that he was a free person and now he could go for a cold beer at the Bee Sting Lounge and then, he winked, they could do something else. When the car left the prison behind them, he gave a loud shout about now being a free man despite his fears about being institutionalized. They were off to the Bee Sting Lounge. When they got there, Brown exited the car along with his Muriel. It was a sand filled parking lot and parking rose quite a bit of dust. They entered the barroom. There were several men sitting at the bar and a few who were sitting at one of the tables. When Brown and his ex-girlfriend, Muriel, came into the barroom, the men in the bar room all stopped doing what they had been doing and the stopped talking. They stared at both of them. Brown took a seat at the bar and ordered a cold beer. Muriel stood in back of him clutching a cold drink in her hand that she had ordered as soon as they both entered the Bee Sting Lounge.

When the beer came, one of the guys who was sitting at the bar said to Brown that he was sick and tired that the prison was so close to the bar and that one or the other should be moved. Brown, who continued to sit there, remained silent. A little while later, Brown responded that he just was released from the prison and that for the first time in a long time he felt free. The man looked at him. He said nothing.

He kept staring at Brown. He knew about prison life since he was a prisoner himself. He had been released from confinement just five years ago. He said that either the prison should be moved or the Bee Sting

Lounge should. Perhaps, the man pointed out, it would be easier to move the Bee Sting Lounge than the prison, but not now. This, apparently, was the wrong thing for the man to say. But we all say things that relate to what is familiar and avoid any reference to the unfamiliar. Apparently, we leave the past alone. He had gotten out of prison only five years ago and prison life was still in his soul. The man who had complained about the location of the prison immediately got up from the barstool where he was sitting and looked sternly at Brown. He told Brown that his grandchildren would have to pay for the prison and that he was intent on not seeing that happen. Nor did he ever imagine going back himself. As far as he was concerned, the prison could stay where it is now and all the prisoners were scum anyhow. All were, except him. We all feel that others are guilty of things that we resent and we are not. When we are wrong, we think we are right, when we are right we think we are wrong. Where did we get this tendency? Probably this feeling that we have cannot be attributed to the way we were raised. Who knows? Other factors probably are much more important.

Both men were silent now. They didn't speak; they simply stared at one another. The man immediately challenged Brown to a fight. That's what people who hang out in bars are expected to do. When they drink too much, they do dumb or stupid things. They brag about what they have done, real or imagined, and they get into fights.

The man was a big man standing well over 6 feet tall, but he was not as muscular as Brown was. Brown had worked out every day that he was in prison. Brown just smiled at the challenge. He had experienced his first physical challenge since he was released from prison, but he was not worried about it. He had many distractors while he was in prison and he met with many challenges. He was not afraid that this one would be any different. He knew that fighting this man would be no match. He didn't understand why everything had to come back to a violent confrontation. People might disagree, but violence was never the answer to anything. But he was not one to avoid a challenge. He cleared his throat and got up from his barstool. Muriel was horrified at this although she continued to stand in back of him.

Both men began to flay at one another. Brown landed the first punch and his opponent went crashing to the floor. His nose was obviously broken; blood was flowing from it all over the floor. Brown knew that this would be the result. It was all over in just a few seconds.

He grabbed Muriel and told her that that they had better leave before the police came. He said to her that a convict would never be free. Not ever, even though the man on the floor was himself a released prisoner. He and Muriel left the Bee Sting barroom with the man still on the floor.

They continued on their way to Muriel's apartment in downtown Boston. The apartment was in the Back Bay section of the City right next to the police station. Brown said that he wondered whether the cops would find out about what he had done at the Bee Sting and whether he would be sent back to prison. Convicts who have been freed from their confinement are usually very pessimistic about everything that they do. They worry and worry that they will be sent back to prison. Even though Brown had wondered if he was institutionalized in prison, he was very happy that he was finally released and that he was in the company of his former girlfriend, Muriel.

"I can't wait to get you alone," he said while still thinking about the man lying on the floor of the Bee Sting barroom.

"Do you remember the guy that I had before you? You were so jealous!" she responded.

Apparently the man whom she made reference to was in her mind and he took care of her physical needs when Brown was first sent to prison. His name was Ralph Mellon. He and Muriel had a very brief affair when Brown was first in prison. They went to her apartment in Boston and they made love. But it was not serious. In fact, nothing serious ever occurred between them. She had been without a man for the time that Brown was in prison. And it bothered her.

When she and Brown finally got to her apartment Brown, after he finished one of the cold beers that Muriel had taken from her refrigerator, moved toward her and grabbed her and he said that he hadn't had a woman in so long that he was not sure how he would react. Pretty soon, however, it was as though he hadn't been away at all; everything worked. He was back to where he was before his prison experience. He had only related to Iota, and only him, when he was in prison at Walpole.

"I know that I'm not being romantic," he said apologetically.

"That's ok," she responded.

They got into bed and had sex. Post coitum omne animal tristde est.

Meanwhile, Iota, back in his cell, missed Brown. He missed cuddling up next to him when he finished reading. This night he went to bed for the evening alone. The guards had finished their work and had gone home. Iota was now alone to his own thoughts. He looked around the cell and saw the place where his own actions had placed him. He looked at the desk where he had done his work and just left. He looked at the book that he had just finished reading. He was glad that he had read it. It was an interesting book he thought. He looked at the sink and the toilet and thought to himself that plenty of people do not have it so well.

Chapter Thirty Two

One day, while Iota was assorting the books in the library, he heard his name being called over the loud speaker. This was the ordinary way that convicts were told that they had visitors. Iota couldn't believe that anyone other than his father would come to visit him. When his father came, they talked about family things and did not have anything to say about Iota being innocent or guilty. His father had been there yesterday and was not expected to return until the following week. Iota continued to calmly put the books away where they belonged and then he proceeded to walk down the hall to the visitors section.

The visitors had all been screened and searched for any contraband. When the visitors first arrived, no matter who they intended to see, they were led into the visitor's area by an armed guard. Before that time, they were herded in a common hallway with the doors closed both in back of them and in front of them. It was not a good thing for a person who was claustrophobic. Afterward, when everything was checked and double checked, they were led into the visitor's area where they met the person whom they had come to visit.

Iota, under guard as was the usual custom, was led to the area where the phones were located. It was necessary for him to be searched, as was one of the customs too, and to follow the same rigid procedures that he had followed when his father came to see him on the previous day. These procedures included the expectation that he would comply with the rule that stated that the prisoner who was being visited would sit on one side of the glass petition where the phones were that separated the visitor and the prisoner. This was the only contact that was allowed between the prisoner and the visitor. The visitor would sit on the other side of the glass, the prisoner on the other. In this way both would be comfortable and each could speak on the phone.

Iota complied with all of these expectations as he took the seat on his side of the glass partition and picked up the phone. He wondered who would come to the prison to visit him as he dangled the phone in front of him.

The visitor on the other side of the glass was Gabriella, the girl that he had known at Savan. She had taken the trip to Walpole because she wanted to see the person who had killed Robert Shaw. There were other motives as well. Secretly, she was fascinated with the killing and she had an attraction to Iota. She thought that he was exceptionally good looking and well built, but didn't want the other girls to know even though the murder of Shaw had occurred over five years ago. But, after speaking with him, she had no hesitation going back to the other girls and telling them that she had visited Iota and that she had indeed spoken to him. She lost her fear of them once she was in the visitors section of the prison.

"My goodness, why are you here?" Iota asked.

"I just came to see you. I thought that it was the nice thing to do."

"Ok, what do you want?"

"Nothing, I just came to see you.

She had accomplished what she had come for; to see him, and after she had seen him, to go back around College where she now lived and lord it over the other ladies that she had done something that they hadn't done in terms of Christian charity. These ladies were highly competitive when it came to Christian charity.

They continued to talk about a number of things. Iota was glad that she had come, but he didn't put too much stock in the visit. He didn't feel the same way that he did when his father came to see him the day before. But he was glad that she had come to Walpole. They continued their banter until time was up. She, half meaning it, said that she would be back again. She left the prison with a self-satisfied look on her face. She immediately went back to Boston to see the other girls.

She told Haley and Samantha what she had done in visiting Iota in prison and what they had talked about. She looked for the other girls but was not able to find them. They were now married and lived in different parts of the city. She told both Haley and Samantha that she had taken the train to Walpole and had visited Iota. The girls were shocked at this and they both said that they wanted to learn more about her visit; what it was like going to a prison and seeing the person who had murdered one of their classmates. They were hungry for anything that Gabriella had to say. Even though they were both shocked that Gabriella would go to the prison at Walpole to see Iota, they didn't respond much. They admired Gabriella for her work in helping people and that she would make the effort to take the train and go see Iota.

"That surprises us," they said almost in unison. "We thought that you didn't like him let aside trains. Thought that you didn't like trains."

She assured the girls that she had gone out of interest and that she had gone because, as a church going Christian, she felt that visiting someone in prison was the right thing to do. Besides, she said that

Iota was not a bad guy. In fact, despite his idiosyncrasies, he could be charming when he wanted to be. He was, as a matter of fact, kind of cute she said. The ladies, Haley and Samantha, were shocked at this, but they accepted what was said and agreed that going to visit someone in prison was a good thing to do and that Iota was essentially a good person. But don't forget, they said, that he was found guilty of the crime of murder.

"We're sorry, but we still think that you shouldn't have gone," they said.

Gabriella smiled but she accepted this. As soon as she started to talk about Iota and what they had spoken about, they were eager to listen. After telling them about the procedure for getting into the prison and how the prison guards had herded the visitors inside a hallway and closed the doors in front of them as well as in back of them, she said that finally they were led into an area where there were a lot of phone banks.

Gabriella told the girls that they had spoken about numerous things. She said that Iota had told her that his father had come to visit on the prior day before she got there and that they had a good visit. She said that Haley and Samantha should both go and visit him. They would feel a bit different if they did.

Iota had told Gabriella that the warden, who was the chief administrative officer, was not a good person at all. Being new at his position, he worried about everything. He was constantly concerned about things that a person in an administrative position should not worry about. Besides, she said, he was a bitter man and had a cruel streak. At least, she said, that's what Iota had told her.

Haley said to her that she understood what Gabriella was saying and that she would have to admit that she found Iota to be attractive too. In fact, she said that she almost dated him. She knew about his homosexuality, in fact she also knew about the relationship that he had with Robert Shaw. Gabriella was taken aback when Haley admitted this and asked her why she hadn't told anyone. When she said that she didn't know, Gabriella decided to drop the entire thing and brought up something else. She spoke about the prison at Walpole and how it must be so difficult for convicts.

CHAPTER THIRTY THREE

Time went on. Prison life was getting to be a routine for Iota. He was getting a bit older. He would get up from his cot, the cot that he shared with Brown, which, for him, was a wonderful experience sharing his bed with another man, and he would answer the call to go to breakfast. He usually had the same breakfast, bacon with scrambled eggs and coffee. Ordinarily, he would sit by himself in the same place in the mess hall, but today he saw a new face, one that he hadn't seen before and decided to sit with him. He went over to where the man was sitting and asked if he could sit there. The man silently nodded his head and Iota sat down.

He asked the man what he was in for. The man began to weep and said that he was in prison because of financial conspiracy that he was involved with. He was sentenced to three years. But he claimed his innocence. Iota didn't know how to respond. He didn't want to appear to others that he favored one person over another; he was satisfied with his position in the prison ever since Brown showed his anger in the shower room. Nor did he want to shun a person who was in need. Both lessons he had learned from Brown. He decided to say only a few things, not everything that he had learned from his nights with Brown or from other convicts.

He told the man that everybody in prison was innocent of the crime that they had been sentenced for and had landed them in prison; that was no surprise. But he said that everyone who did make it did so by accepting their fate. Besides, he said that while nobody really chose to be in prison, life here was not so bad. A person could land up in another jail, at Attica or Sing Sing. Here you get three meals a day, change in clothing every other day, a relatively comfortable place to sleep, [he didn't mention his relationship with Brown], a job that one likes; things could be worse he told him. Life outside is so predictable, he said to the man. First you get excited about a job, then you do it and it becomes routine, an expected part of your life. You get up in the morning, do your thing and then drive home, sometimes traveling long distances between work and where your home is. Being in prison, you don't have to worry about driving long distances. You're already here. It's a great deal better than worrying about things like driving long distances or where you next meal is coming from or where you're going to sleep tonight or if you're going to be fired. It's a lot worse if you're homeless. He continued the conversation along these lines until the other man stopped his weeping.

The other man told him that his name was Jim, Jim Casey. When Iota told him that he was not interested in his name, only that he began to see the wisdom of his being there and accepting it, the man responded that he felt better now, knowing that he had a friend. Unbeknownst to Iota he was also a gay person. Iota, thinking that he had done something good for the day, was pleased with himself and what he had said to Casey. He excused himself and went about his own business.

He went back to his cell, picked up the book that he had finished reading to take it back to the library, straighten up his cot, cleaned up as much as possible and headed off to the library. Before he got there, he was met again by James Casey. When Iota asked him if there was something else that he could do for him, Casey told him, in a voice that was hardly more than a whisper, that he was gay himself. He said that he knew about Iota from the other convicts who had been in the shower area when Iota's friend told them to forget about what they were thinking and that they would have to answer to him if they didn't. The guys thought that it would be best if they complied since Iota's friend was so big and so tough looking. They thought that it would be better for them to look for someone else to take care of their needs. Casey said that he was afraid that they would find out about him and that they would abuse him because of it.

In addition, Iota told him that most of the convicts masturbate in order to achieve sexual satisfaction. He told him that the word "masturbation" came from two Latin words, manus and struprare which literally means to rape with the hand.

Iota thought for a moment and he told Casey that he could share his cell and his cot with him just as Brown did before he was released from prison. Casey smiled a half smile at Iota's invitation and asked him if anybody, for example the warden, would mind. When Iota told him that nobody would mind at all, that the assignment of cells was purely arbitrary and that the same thing is true about who shares cots with whom.

Casey broke into a wide smile.

CHAPTER THIRTY FOUR

T ime flew by as it does for everyman. Iota's hair was almost completely white and there were "crow's feet" on his face that showed how completely he had aged. Both Brown and Casey had gone and were only distant memories to him. However, he thought about them often and he smiled when he did. He remembered the nights when he would cuddle next to Brown and then to Casey when Brown had been released and the thoughts of both of them brought a smile to his face. Otherwise, he was a Stoic figure to most of the men who were in prison with him.

One day, in early spring, he was called to the warden's office. After praising his work in the library, the warden asked him if he had heard anything in the prison yard. Anything that could be interpreted as plans to escape. The warden was constantly worried that one or more of his charges would try to break out of the prison. He apparently had not forgotten the one or two men who had tried to escape in the past. The prison psychologists said that he was obsessed with this possibility. The psychologists were very concerned about him and his mental health.

Iota simply smiled at this suggestion, got up from the chair that the warden had provided for him, excused himself and went to the library for another day's work. When he got there, a gaggle of prisoners were waiting to see him. They, to a man, said that they wanted to take advantage of the prison's offer to send books back home for others to read. They all had kids at home whom they had neglected prior to their stay at Walpole. They felt that by sending the books home they would be doing a sort of penance and that people at home would forgive them for their transgressions. Not that they had asked the people back home how they felt about their being in prison but it was not unusual for convicts, when they had any chance to show contriteness, to behave in this manner. Iota didn't mind. It gave him something to do during the day rather than to sit and read as was his usual custom.

He took several books from the shelves and gave them to his fellow prisoners. He kept doing the same thing until most of the library books were in the possession of the prisoners. With most of the books in the hands of the prisoners, the library looked empty; its shelves were now depleted. The prisoners who now had books to send home didn't seem to mind about the empty shelves. Most of them were not readers; they simply wanted to send the books that they now possessed back home for their kids to read.

Iota looked happy. He was pleased that they wanted to send home what he had recommended to the library committee all these years. He had fought very diligently for a program where the prisoners could send books home and not feel any guilt about it. Now he had realized what he had pleaded for in front of the committee.

He felt good. He decided, after the prisoners had left, to go for a little walk. He had many privileges that the other prisoners did not have because of his age and good conduct. Working in the library didn't hurt either.

It was a good day to be outside in the prison yard. Nature had exploded into a lush springtime show of her determination. The streams of sunlight crashed through the clouds that had covered the sky and crocuses were bellowing their spring song and showing their tiny heads. Tulips were standing still beside the walls of the prison playing the part of silent sentinels to the warden's office. The guards on the walls were anxious and had their rifles pointed at Iota. They were instructed to not allow anybody access to the prison walls. When Iota waved, they recognized who it was and they put their rifles down.

Iota finished his walk without further ado, and went inside the prison walls again. He strolled through the hallway where the warden's office was like he belonged there. He often would go unannounced to the warden's office. Newer convicts, or those who were in bad terms with the warden, were not permitted to even go into the office unescorted. They would be punished if they did. Most of the new convicts understood this. Those who were there for a considerable period of time and who had done something that the warden had not approved of understood the punishment system. To go someplace that the warden called his own was highly verboten and they did not dare to break from his expectations that this was his space; his very own space. But one that Iota and other trusted convicts had access to. The prisoners accepted whatever punishment that the warden handed out when a violation occurred. He was fair despite his own personality infirmities. One of these infirmities was allowing Iota reign over what was essentially the wardens.

Iota was taken aside by one of the guards and informed that he had a visitor. Slowly, he scratched his head wondering who the visitor was. When he could not figure out who the visitor might be, he went to the room where they had the phone banks. He wondered who would be visiting him at this time. Who would come to visit an old man who had so little time left in this world. He sat down and took a phone in his hand after he greeted the guards with a warm hello. He waited for the visitor, whoever it was, to take the phone on the other side of the petition.

The visitor was Arthur Pierce. Pierce was an old man himself. He still had wavy hair, but it was as white as snow now and he walked with agony in each step. He was happy to sit down and take the phone.

"What the hell are you doing here?" Iota asked him.

He answered Iota's question by saying that he had a sudden urge to see the man who had murdered Robert Shaw, one of his students when he first began teaching. He said that he couldn't really retire until he was sure of the guilt of the person who had taken Shaw's life. He had retired nearly two years ago, but his retirement was filled with anger and anxiety at Shaw's death. In addition, as a Christian, he thought that visiting a man in prison was the right thing to do. They spoke about these and other things that had bothered Pierce.

The conversation quickly turned to other stuff. They spoke about Savan College, its success in the recent basketball tournament and the activities that it had now in contrast to when Pierce began to teach. They both laughed at many of the changes that had taken place since the time when Pierce started teaching there. Iota asked him about his final classes before he took the plunge and announced that indeed he had planned to retire. He was genuinely interested in what Pierce had to say.

Pierce said that his final class went smoothly. It was no different than any other class that he taught. He had given the students the word of the day and a famous person's expression as well as the outline that he would use to spell out the lecture that he gave that day as he always did. He was noted for his outlines. The students took turns praising them and then decrying them. But they were always frank and ultimately said nice things the effort that he had put into them. He then asked Iota about his stay in Walpole. He told Iota that he was not at Walpole to discuss his knack of giving the students his thoughts, but was interested in how Iota was doing.

Iota said that prison life was not that bad; for him anyhow. He told Pierce about Brown and Casey. He said that his relationship was different for both of them. With Brown he felt protected when they both cuddled in bed. With Casey, it was a bit different. Casey was so dependent on him.

"How do you mean?" Pierce asked

"Well, I don't know. I guess I mean that Brown was one way and Casey was opposite."

"What do you mean?" Pierce was getting really interested in what Iota was saying.

"I think that I mean that with Brown I always felt secure even when we showered. With Casey I had a different feeling. He was so dependent. I guess what I'm saying is that when we went to bed in the evening he was not very responsive. I guess that's it."

"I understand."

"Do you? When Casey related to me, I knew there was something wrong. He never said that he agreed with me about so many things. He didn't agree that life in prison was better than life on the streets. I told him that at other prisons, life may be more difficult. At places like Sing Sing or Attica, life is much more difficult. You are punished for the slightest infraction. If he had gone there, he might have a reason to say that life in prison was not the life that he had wanted for himself.

"Despite the fact that we didn't have the opportunity to do many of the things that we could do on the outside, life in this prison is not a bad way to live. I told him that there was any number of things that we prisoners benefited from, from medical care to going to the dentist.

And we don't have to be bored by anything. Everything is exciting here. Usually when things happen on the outside, you can't help falling into a routine and routines are boring. You get bored. Even if you have a great deal of dough, it becomes boring. Money doesn't change the way you feel or think about things.

There are opportunities to learn a craft or a skill with all the shops that they have built. They still are in the process of building other ones. They teach the cons so many skills. People on the outside don't have these opportunities.

When it comes to travel, I have all the cites in the world in National Geographic. Most people get kind of bored with where there at. I don't. I can look at any country in the world and be surprised at their geography and history. I guess you would answer me by saying that most people are not like me. I guess you are right.

You have medical services whenever you need them including dental care, you get three meals a day, a decent job, for me at least. You don't have to worry about traffic or anything that deals with a car like getting gasoline at the service station or the family car getting older. You get to write in the evening or read a book. There are plenty of things that give lie to the commonly assumed definition that prison life is not consistent with living a good life. Think of your teaching. Think for a moment about it. It gets boring, doesn't it? You don't live your life according to an outline. You don't concern yourself with the word of the day or expressions or the outlines that you spend so much time on. Do you?"

"No, I guess not But what about Shaw?" Pierce responded.

"Life in prison is not bad at all. Even for a lifer like me, especially for a lifer like me. Even when it comes to sex. I have a good sex life. But what about a guy who is heterosexual? Especially if he is a religious. Does this make a difference? I don't know the answer to that question." He ignored the question of Shaw.

"But I came here to talk about Shaw not prison life."

They continued to converse with each other. Iota made several points that Pierce didn't argue about. He told Pierce about the new chapel where he went to pray. He had become religious the older he got. He recognized that his life left quite a bit to mend spiritually and the new chapel gave him the opportunity to focus on that. He was surprised that they hadn't built one before. He felt that his life was better now with his developing spirituality. He thought about God frequently and about Christ. Whether this was related to his knowledge of death or not is up in the air.

Also, the prison had begun to construct new facilities for basketball. Apparently, they recognized the importance of men playing games and they were in the process of construction new courts in at least two parts of the prison that were previously used as warehouses for equipment and storage. The old game facility had lost its appeal to the men and its dirty evidence was forever a thing of the past.

Pierce said his goodbyes to Iota and left the visitor's area. He walked with unsteady gait as he promised that he would come back to see him although he knew that this was a lie. He had come primarily to speak to Iota about Shaw, but somehow Iota had focused on his own life and on the prison.

Pierce did take a kind of delight in talking to Iota though. He, in fact, enjoyed the conversation that they had. Pierce was not a talkative man. Iota had made some interesting observations about prison life. Whether he agreed or disagreed with Iota's observations about prison life and the evidence that Iota had about it was neither here nor there. Most of the arguments that Iota had made about prison life were good observations Pierce thought. From Iota's perspective, the arguments that he had made sense, at least to him they did. To somebody in another prison they may not have, but to Iota that was irrelevant.

Pierce was very quiet. He was quite when it came to expressing his ideas at Savan. He hardly ever began a conversation with his colleagues.

When issues were raised, he remained quiet. He didn't like talking. Perhaps that is why he was so well liked.

He left Walpole's prison waving at the guards in their watch towers. The springtime breeze fumbled with his aging body and his white hair.